Fin
Answers
by

Kathi Daley

This book is a work of fiction. Names, characters, places, and incidents either are products of the author's imagination or are used fictitiously. Any resemblance to actual events or locales or persons, living or dead, is entirely coincidental.

Copyright © 2018 by Katherine Daley

Version 1.0

All rights reserved, including the right of reproduction in whole or in part in any form.

Chapter 1

Monday, June 18

He watched the boy skipping rocks across the clear, still water. From the cover of dense forest, he listened to the childish squeals of delight as the flat, hard surface of the stone met the firm, unyielding force of the lake. Each hop resulted in an ever-widening web of rings, each ring larger yet less intense than the one that came before. Life, he mused, was like those rings. The farther you traveled from the point of origin, the wider your reach, but the less intense the effect. He'd spent a lifetime struggling to affect change in the larger rings, but now, he'd decided, it was time to avenge the iniquities of his past, to claim the inner ring as his own.

Vinnie Truman had been missing for just over an hour. The four-year-old with the sandy blond hair, big green eyes, and a smattering of freckles had been playing with his eight-year-old brother, Kip, and six-year-old sister, Cammie, in the yard of the cabin his parents, Jim and Joan, had rented for their summer vacation. No one saw Vinnie wander away. No one could explain why he would have.

Both Jim and Joan swore they'd been keeping an eye on their children as they grilled burgers on the deck just off the kitchen. When we walked in, Joan had been telling Officer Houston that she'd only looked away for a minute and had no idea how Vinnie could simply have disappeared.

"She's lying," I whispered to my partner, Jake Cartwright, the Rescue, Alaska Search and Rescue captain.

"Why do you say that?" Jake asked, his eyes narrowing as he scanned the room, seemingly taking in the climate around us.

I looked toward the short blond woman who was wringing her hands in distress as she clung to the sturdy arm of the uniformed officer she was speaking to. "Her blouse is buttoned wrong, her feet are bare, and her hair is mussed. There may have been grilling going on, but it wasn't in the kitchen, and they weren't focused on their children."

Jake snorted, I was sure, to suppress a chuckle. "Play nice," he whispered as he stepped forward to greet the officer in charge.

"You got here fast," Hank Houston, a tall, broad-shouldered man with chiseled features, dark hair, dark eyes, and a serious way about him, commented as he reached out to Jake.

"We were in the area," Jake responded as he shook the man's hand.

"This is Jim and Joan Truman," Houston introduced the obviously distressed couple. "And this is Jake Cartwright from Rescue, Alaska."

"Don't worry. We're going to do everything we can to find your boy," Jake said, his voice gentle. He turned and gestured to me and the two dogs with us. "This is my teammate, Harmony Carson, and our canine helpers, Sitka and Yukon."

"Officer Houston said he called for the search-and-rescue *team*," Joan said through her tears. "There are only two of you." I could see the woman was on the verge of hysteria, which could only serve to make the situation worse. "He's just a little boy. He could be injured and is probably scared. Two just won't do."

"There are a half dozen police officers looking for your boy," Houston assured her. "The search-and-rescue squad is well trained and familiar with the area. They can cover a lot of ground with just a few people and are here to lend a hand. I can assure you, ma'am, we're doing everything we can to find Vinnie."

Jake turned and looked at Joan. I watched the hard lines of his face soften as he took her hand in his. He'd been doing this a long time. He knew what to do: offer hope but get what you needed. "Harmony and I were running training exercises in the area when the call came in, so we came straight over, but we have four other highly trained members of our team in transit. We'll do everything in our power to find your boy."

Joan's face softened slightly as I imagined her clinging to that promise. I watched as she smiled slightly at Jake and then looked doubtfully toward the dogs. "Can they find him? That one looks so young."

Jake's hand visibly tightened on Joan's. "Yukon is still a puppy, but he's been doing very well with his training, and Sitka is a veteran search-and-rescue dog. He has dozens of rescues under his belt. He's one of the best at what he does, and I know he'll do his very best to find your boy. We're going to need your help, however. The most important thing you can do now is to stay strong. Can you do that?"

The woman nodded.

"Okay, good." Jake shot her a look of approval. That seemed to calm her somewhat. "First, I'll need a recent photo of Vinnie."

The man Houston had introduced as Vinnie's father handed Jake a photo he'd been holding since we'd arrived. Jake looked at it, then handed it to me. I tried to ignore the noise in the room and focus on the curious eyes and crooked grin of the boy we'd been tasked to find.

"I'll need a couple of pieces of clothing Vinnie's worn," Jake added. "The more recently they were worn, the better. Perhaps his pajamas."

"I'll get them," Vinnie's dad said, seeming grateful for something to do.

Jake nodded at him, then turned his attention back to Vinnie's mother. "How long have you been staying at this cabin?"

"Almost a week." She ran a hand over her face.

"And I understand Vinnie has been missing about an hour?" Jake continued.

Vinnie's mother nodded. "Yes. We tried looking for him ourselves for a while before we called the police."

Jake continued. "Is there anywhere you've walked in the past week that seemed to fascinate Vinnie? Anywhere he might want to return to?"

Vinnie's mother shook her head. "No. He was supposed to stay in the yard. I only looked away for a minute."

Jake looked at me. "Are you picking up anything?"

I shook my head. "Not yet." Jake didn't bother to explain to Jim and Joan that I was often able to connect with people I was destined to help rescue. It certainly wasn't an exact science, and I wasn't always able to do it, but I felt as emotionally connected to the child in the photo as I felt irritated by the woman who'd been canoodling with her husband rather than watching her children.

"Where was the last place you saw your son, ma'am?" I asked as I tried to get a visual image that could help me to get a read on the boy.

"I don't know. I can't remember. It happened so suddenly." The woman was gesturing wildly with her hands, as if to make me, to make us all, understand. "One minute he was there and the next he was gone." A fresh stream of tears started down the woman's face. "I only looked away for a minute."

"So you've said," I responded as I glanced down at the photo once again. I know it isn't my job to judge the actions of the people we're tasked to help, and I didn't have children, so I wasn't an expert when it came to the supervision of the under-ten crowd, but what I did know was that if I ever did have a child, which was highly unlikely, I wouldn't leave him or her unattended in the Alaskan wilderness.

"You'll find my boy?" Vinnie's mother pleaded after I glanced up from the photo.

"We'll try," I answered. The team I belonged to was one of the best anywhere, our survival record unmatched. Still, I'd learned at an early age that when you're battling Mother Nature, even the best teams occasionally came out on the losing end. I looked at Jake. "I'm going to head outside with the dogs. I might have better luck in a quiet environment."

After leaving the house, I sat down on a bench and instructed both dogs to sit at my feet. Sitka was an old pro at this sort of thing and waited patiently for the hunt to begin, while Yukon, sensing that something important was up, danced around on the end of his lead. I scratched him behind the ears before instructing him, again, to sit and wait. Thankfully, he did. Yukon had so much raw talent, I was certain he was going to be as good a search-and-rescue dog as Sitka eventually, but he was less than a year old and, at times, still easily distracted.

Once Yukon settled into the wait position next to Sitka, I closed my eyes and took a deep breath. I'm not sure why I'm able to connect psychically with those I'm meant to rescue. It isn't that I can feel the pain of everyone who's suffering; it seems to be only those we're meant to help that find their way onto my radar. I'm not entirely sure where the ability comes from, but I know when I acquired it. When I was seventeen, my sister Val, who was also my legal guardian after our parents' death in a car accident, went out on a rescue. She got lost in a storm, and although the team tried to find her, they came up with nothing but dead ends. I remember sitting at the command post, praying harder than I ever had. I wanted so much to have the chance to tell Val how much I loved her and, suddenly, there she was, in my head. I could feel her pain, but I also felt the prayer in her heart. I knew she was dying, but I could feel her love for me as her life slipped away. I'd tried to tell the others I knew where she was, but they'd thought my ramblings were those of an emotionally distraught teenager dealing with the fallout of shock and despair. When the team eventually found Val's body exactly where and how I'd told them they would, they began to believe I'd made a connection with the only family I'd had left in the world.

Since then, I've used my gift to locate and rescue dozens of people. I couldn't save them all, but today, I was determined that our search for Vinnie would result in a check in the Save column. I tried to focus on the image of the child with the mischievous grin. I sensed water and was picking up the feeling of curiosity rather than fear. That was good. Chances are, as I suspected, the boy had wandered off chasing a rabbit or some other small creature and hadn't even realized he was lost yet. It was a warm day, and Vinnie's mother had assured us that he wore jeans, tennis shoes, and a hooded sweatshirt, so at least we didn't have the elements to worry about, as we did with so many of the winter rescues on which we were called out.

I heard Yukon begin to whine. I opened my eyes and saw team members Wyatt Forrester, Dani Matthews, Landon Stanford, and Austin Brown walking toward us. Yukon stood up, preparing to greet some of his favorite people.

"Sit and wait," I reminded the pup.

He plopped his butt on the ground but continued to wag his tail. Beside him, Sitka thumped his tail without having moved an inch.

The group stopped several feet short of the dogs. The animals were working, so playful scratches and enthusiastic kisses would have to wait.

"Any news?" Dani asked.

"Jake is inside, talking to the parents. I'm sure he'll be out soon. I haven't been able to establish a clear connection to the boy, but I sense water near his current location. I don't think he realizes he's lost. I sense curiosity but not fear."

Wyatt was about to say something when Jake walked out of the house with two plastic bags, each containing a piece of clothing Vinnie had worn.

"Anything?" Jake asked me.

I told him what I'd just told the others.

"There are two bodies of water nearby," Jake said. "Eagle Lake is about a half mile up the mountain and Glacier Lake is about a half mile down the mountain from here." Jake looked around, as if sizing up the situation. "The family has hiked in both directions within the past twenty-four hours. It's likely the dogs will pick up the boy's scent in either direction, at least initially. We'll divide into two groups. I'll take Sitka, Dani, and Austin and head up the mountain. Harmony and Yukon can work with Wyatt and Landon and head toward the lower lake." Jake looked at me. "If Yukon picks up a strong scent, radio and we can discuss a strategy. If you make a stronger connection to Vinnie, or are able to pick up anything more specific, let us know."

Jake, as Sitka's handler, and me, as Yukon's, each took a plastic bag. Once we'd cleared the yard, we let our dogs sniff the piece of clothing, telling them repeatedly, "This is Vinnie; find Vinnie." When the dogs seemed to understand what it was we were asking, we took them off their leads, then followed. I trailed directly behind Yukon, while Wyatt walked parallel to my route to the right and Landon paralleled to the left.

Once Sitka had a scent, he was usually very focused on the task at hand, so the odds of Jake and his team finding Vinnie if he had traveled up the mountain were great. Yukon, on the other hand, was pretty green. He had been abandoned on my doorstep five months earlier, and I, as I always did, had taken him in. Over the course of the next month, I'd worked to teach him the house rules. During his training, I'd noticed what I felt was an innate ability to find whatever it was I sent him to look for. I spoke to Jake, and he agreed to help me train him for search and rescue. We'd discussed needing a second dog. Yukon caught on to the training like a fish to water, and although he'd only been training for a few months, he'd already been successful in locating the victim in five different simulations. Of course, a real rescue was a lot more intense than a simulation for both dog and handler, and this was the first time he'd participated in a real rescue without Sitka by his side to show him how it was done.

Yukon headed into the dense foliage of the nearby forest and I followed. I glanced at Wyatt, who was perhaps fifty yards to my right, and then Landon, who was fifty yards to my left. They nodded, letting me know they were able to follow despite the rough terrain. I glanced at Yukon, who sniffed the air and headed deeper into the forest. While we searched, I kept an eye on him, but basically let him do his thing. After several minutes, he alerted, showing interest where a fallen tree blocked the path. "Did you find something?" Yukon sniffed the log and wagged his tail. "Good boy." I looked around and called Vinnie's name. Nothing. I stood perfectly still and closed my eyes. I waited for a vision to appear. I could sense the boy, and, as before, he didn't seem frightened. But there was something. Something dark. Something menacing. I tried to hone in on it, but I couldn't get a clear reading, so I tied a flag to a tree branch to mark the spot, then took the pajama top out of the bag. I once again held it under Yukon's nose. "This is Vinnie. Find Vinnie." Yukon set off down the trail. I went after him.

I knew once Vinnie realized he was lost, fear would overcome him. That would help me to connect with him, yet I hoped for his sake we'd find him before he became terrified. The forest was thick with evergreens and underbrush. Yukon had left the trail after we'd come across the fallen log, which meant Vinnie most likely had left the trail as well. The area was home to a variety of wildlife, including grizzlies, wolves, and cougars. It was dangerous for anyone to veer off the established trail, but it was especially dangerous for little boys who had no idea that danger lurked in the dark places beyond the clearing.

It wasn't easy to both follow Yukon and focus on Vinnie. If we didn't either hear from Jake or find him in the next few minutes, I'd call to the dog to take a break.

As we approached the lake, Yukon alerted again. As before, I stopped and looked around. I called for Vinnie and then listened. I closed my eyes and tried desperately to make a connection. This time, the vision was a bit clearer. Vinnie had stopped what he was doing to look around. He must have realized he was lost and, as predicted, curiosity had been replaced by fear.

"Harmony to Jake," I said through the radio.

"Go ahead."

"I have a vision. He's near Glacier Lake."

"We're on our way."

I closed my eyes and focused again. He was terrified. Fear and panic fueled the boy as he ran through the underbrush. I cringed as I saw him trip over something. Pain. Now the fear was mingled with pain. He got up and tried to run, but the pain was too much. When he fell again, he simply sat on the ground, clutching his ankle and screaming for help. I took a deep breath. There was something else. Darkness. Danger.

I opened my eyes and looked at Yukon. "Find Vinnie. We need to find Vinnie." I gave him another sniff of the pajama top and waited. He sniffed the air, then took off at a run. I tried unsuccessfully to keep up with him and was about to call him back when I heard three sharp barks.

"Vinnie," I called as loudly as I could.

"Here. I'm here."

I headed down the trail as quickly as I could manage. Sprawled on the ground was a terrified little boy with his arms around Yukon, who gently licked the tears from his face.

"Good boy," I said to Yukon. I knelt next to Vinnie. "Are you hurt?"

"My ankle. I hurt my ankle."

I radioed Jake to let him know I'd found Vinnie. He would need to be carried back to the cabin, so I waited for Wyatt and Landon to catch up.

"Other than your ankle, do you hurt anywhere?" I asked.

The boy shook his head. He was smiling now that Yukon had settled in next to him. "I was lost. I was on the trail, but then I looked around and nothing looked right. I was so scared. I ran as fast as I could. I wanted to get home, but then I fell."

I looked back the way Vinnie had traveled. "Did you trip on a log?"

Vinnie wiped the tears from his dirt-streaked face. "I don't know. I didn't see."

"Help is on the way. We'll get you home in no time. You're safe now."

"Mama will be mad. I'm not supposed to leave the yard." The boy began to sob. "I'm going to get a time-out. I hate time-outs."

I pulled my sweatshirt over my head and used it to wipe away the boy's tears. "I can't say for certain, but I think your mom will be so happy to see you that she might forget to be mad. Still, the rule about staying in the yard is a good one. You could have been in real trouble if Yukon hadn't found you. There are all sorts of things out here that can hurt a little boy."

"Like bears?"

I nodded. "Yes, like bears. And cougars, and wolves, and all sorts of animals that might be lurking nearby, waiting to attack."

The boy began to sob hysterically. Yukon began to lick his face frantically to offer comfort. Okay, so maybe I oversold the danger angle. I didn't mean to traumatize the kid; I just wanted him to understand the potential consequences of his actions.

"What's wrong?" Wyatt said, arriving in the nick of time as far as I was concerned. He bent down and picked the boy up in his arms. "Are you hurt?"

"No." The boy began to hiccup from hysteria.

"So why all the tears?"

"I was bad and a bear might have ate me."

Wyatt looked at me and raised a brow.

I lifted a shoulder. "It's not like I have experience talking to kids. Dogs are more my thing."

Wyatt winked at me. "You did good. Yukon too. Let's get this scared little boy back to his parents."

"Wait," I said as Wyatt turned to head back to the cabin. I stood up and slowly scanned the forest as Landon arrived. I could still sense the darkness I'd picked up before. I couldn't identify what I was feeling, but an iciness settled into my chest. I felt pain and hopelessness and death. "There's someone else. Someone near death." I closed my eyes and concentrated. The image of a man's face filtered through my mind, but it was blurry and out of focus. It was as if the man was passing in and out of consciousness, letting me in and then pushing me out. "Oh God," I whispered.

"What is it?" Wyatt asked. "What do you see?"

I glanced at Vinnie, who looked scared to death. I tried to level my voice despite the intense grief that had gripped my body. "Go ahead and take Vinnie back to his parents. Landon, Yukon, and I will try to find the source of my vision."

Wyatt looked uncertain, but he didn't argue. He nodded and began walking back toward the cabin. When he was out of sight, I closed my eyes and tried to see the face of the man again. Landon stood quietly next to me, holding Yukon's lead. He took my hand in his free one and held on tight. He'd been with me long enough to know how draining this was for me.

"Anything?" Landon asked in a voice so soft I barely heard him.

"It isn't focused. It's a man. I can't see his face. He's hurt. His image is fading in and out. He doesn't want to let me in." My breath caught as I connected just in time to experience what I was sure was the man's last breath. I shook my head, then opened my eyes. "He's gone."

"Where?"

I looked through the dense forest. "I don't know. I wasn't linked for more than a few seconds. He was resisting, but I managed to connect right at the end, when his only choice was to surrender. Now that he's dead I can't sense him." I looked around at the thick trees. "We'll need help to find him." I radioed Jake and informed him of the situation, then Landon, Yukon, and I began to search for the man I had seen in my mind.

Jake's dog, Sitka, had been trained to find missing people as well as those who had already passed on. Yukon was training to follow a specific scent, as we'd just done with Vinnie, but he had no training as a cadaver dog. Our best bet at finding the man whose death I had just experienced was to force myself to remember everything about that moment. Everything I had seen, heard, smelled, and felt.

"The man was lying on the ground," I said in a soft voice. "He was cold. Weak. Wet, perhaps. He was partially covered, but the purpose of the cover wasn't to provide warmth but camouflage."

"You said wet? Is he near the water?" Landon asked.

"Maybe. It's dark. The trees in the area are dense." I opened my eyes and scanned the area. I could remember the pain, the fear, the urge to fight, and then the peace that came with the decision to give in and float away from the world toward whatever came next.

"Are you okay?" Landon asked.

I nodded.

Landon used his thumb to wipe a tear from my cheek. "I know it's painful."

"It's okay. I'm okay," I assured him. There are times I want to run from the images and feelings that threaten to overwhelm and destroy me, but I know embracing the pain and the fear is my only path to the answers I seek. "In the last moment of his life, there was fear, anger, and pain, but something else as well." I focused harder. "Acceptance and," I tried to remember, "penance. He was sorry for something he did and with his last breath was seeking forgiveness."

"From whom?" Landon asked.

I opened my eyes. "I don't know. Maybe God. Maybe himself. Maybe someone he'd wronged." I continued to scan the forest, looking for something familiar. The only thing I could see in my vision was trees, which didn't help me a bit because there were trees everywhere.

"Do you remember anything from your vision that will help us know where to look?" Landon asked again. "Anything at all that will help us narrow things down?"

"There were trees and it was dark." I took a breath and forced my mind to calm and focus. "The ground was gently sloped and covered with wild grass." I bit my lip as I tried to get a feeling for direction. "There." I pointed into the distance.

Landon set off in the direction I indicated with Yukon at his side. I followed closely behind. Shortly after we'd entered the densest part of the forest, Yukon began to whine.

"Do you have the scent?"

Yukon barked three times.

"Let him go," I instructed Landon. "He may not be trained to retrieve those who have passed on, but he's a dog and better able to pick up scent than either of us."

It didn't take long. No longer, really, than it took to take a breath for Yukon to find the body. I felt my knees weaken and my stomach lurch. "It's Pastor Brown." I gasped as Landon bent down and took a closer look at the man who was partially covered by the thick underbrush.

"If only we'd been a few minutes sooner," I said to Landon as he pulled away the vines and ferns that someone seemed to have arranged from the man's body. He knelt and felt for a pulse, then shook his head. The pastor's throat had been slit and he had a piece of duct tape across his mouth.

"He couldn't even scream," I said, as if that somehow made it worse.

"I wonder how he got here," Landon said.

I felt the hairs on the back of my neck stand up. Yukon began to growl from deep in his chest as I scanned our surroundings. I didn't see or hear anything, but my intuition told me that Pastor Brown's killer was still nearby. "Someone brought him here. Someone who's still here."

Landon stood up and looked around. "I don't see anything. Are you sure you sense a second person?"

"I'm not a hundred percent sure, but I do sense someone. I don't feel as if he's a threat to us, though. I'll call Jake to have him fill Officer Houston in on what we've found."

I made the call, then returned my attention to Landon, who was still standing over the body. We both knew not to touch him because we could destroy evidence, but in that moment not touching was very difficult indeed. I'd felt the man's life leave his body. There was a voice in my head that demanded I do something better than simply stand there.

"It looks like he'd been swimming," I said. He was soaking wet, but he was fully dressed, and it was much too cold to have gone swimming in a lake whose source was melting snow, so the idea was probably ridiculous.

"I doubt that, but he is wet," Landon replied. He nodded to the pastor's bloody wrists without touching him. "It looks like he was bound at some point, though there are no signs of any ropes here."

"Maybe he was tossed from a boat and swam to shore," I suggested. "Once he made it to land, the cold-blooded killer who dumped him in the water slit his throat and left him to die."

"Maybe," Landon replied. "Someone tried to camouflage the body. I'm guessing he'd passed out before he died. Maybe he *was* tossed from a boat and swam to shore before he was killed." Landon paused and turned his head. "It sounds like the others are almost here."

Chapter 2

After Officer Houston and his men showed up to take possession of the body, the search-and-rescue team headed toward Neverland, the bar Jake owned, for a debriefing. The team consisted of eight full-time members and a handful of on-call members, in addition to Sitka and Yukon. The full-time members, in addition to myself, included Jake, who had been at the game the longest and was considered by all to be the leader of the pack; Sarge, retired military and Jake's full-time cook at Neverland; Austin, the newest member of the team and a local firefighter; Landon, a computer genius and the uncontested brains of the team; Wyatt, an eternal child, an unapologetic playboy, second in command to Jake, and a serious mountain climber and backcountry skier; Dani, an intense individual, a helicopter owner, and a backcountry hiker; and Jordan Fairchild, Jake's current love interest and a local doctor who hadn't been involved in today's rescue.

The first thing I noticed when entering Neverland was the fantastic smell coming from the kitchen. Sarge wasn't only one of the sweetest people I'd ever met but a hell of a cook and a master at the command post.

"What smells so good?" I asked after hanging my jacket on one of the hooks provided for that purpose.

"Jake called to let me know the team was on the way, so I tossed some sausages, peppers, and onions on the grill. I have freshly baked rolls for sandwiches and potato salad as well."

"Sounds good. I'm starving."

"I'll dish everything up and bring it out while you're all getting settled," Sarge offered.

As soon as Landon arrived, he began to record the details of the search into the logbook we kept as a history of sorts. In addition to the name of the search victim, the team members who responded, the time, date, duration, and topographical and weather conditions of the search, facts such as the health and well-being of the victim at the time of the rescue and any other special circumstances were recorded. I knew today's debrief would focus almost exclusively on the special circumstance of discovering the body of one of Rescue's most prominent citizens.

"So, what do we know?" Wyatt asked Jake once he completed the phone call he'd been involved in when we arrived and settled in with the rest of us.

Jake began. "Pastor Brown's body was found in the forest near Glacier Lake by Harmony and her team during a routine rescue operation. It appeared his wrists had been bound at some point, although no ropes were found at the scene, and the duct tape over his mouth appeared to have been there for quite some time. If I had to guess, his hands were bound right up to the point when he died because the wounds were raw and oozing blood. Based on the evidence found, or more precisely not found, at the scene, Officer Houston believed he was abducted elsewhere and then brought to the lake, where his throat was slit. While the crime scene guys are still considering all scenarios, it appeared he was forced into the water, or maybe he tried to escape by diving into the water. It's unclear at this point how he got wet, although it does appear as if his throat was slit after he'd left the water." Jake paused and took a breath. "At this point, Officer Houston doesn't have a theory as to why Pastor Brown was abducted, or when it happened. We're assuming he wasn't gone long because no missing person report had been filed."

"He lives alone," I said. "With the exception of Sundays, special events, and holidays, he has a fairly solitary job. It's possible he was missing since after services on Sunday and no one realized it."

"Houston is going to interview Pastor Brown's secretary as well as his neighbors to determine when he was taken. What we do know is that he was killed this morning. Houston said it was lucky for Vinnie that he didn't wander down to the beach any earlier than he did. Houston estimates Vinnie missed being a witness to the murder by less than thirty minutes, and given the fact that Harmony sensed the pastor was still alive when Vinnie was found, I'd say it was even less."

The idea that Vinnie could have stumbled onto a situation that could very well have resulted in his own death sent a chill down my spine. I had to wonder if he had heard or seen anything. I wondered if anyone had asked him.

"Houston is operating under the assumption that the killer took off immediately after killing Brown and most likely was gone before Vinnie arrived," Jake continued. "The CSI team is at the site looking for footprints, evidence of a boat, and any other clues that might have been left behind."

"No," I said, almost without realizing I had spoken.

Jake looked at me. "No?"

I lifted my eyes and studied the others sitting at the table. "No, the killer didn't leave right away," I said. "I felt him. When we first arrived, even before we got there, I sensed his presence. I couldn't see his face, but I was overcome with darkness." I looked directly at Jake. "I think he was there. Watching."

"Are you sure?"

I nodded.

"Harmony did seem to pick up both the killer and the victim," Landon verified.

"I couldn't see the man, but I could feel his thoughts," I continued. "Not all of them. Just random things passing through his mind. He was fascinated by what he'd done, and sorry the boy was there. He thought of leaving when the boy arrived, but his need to experience grief made him stay." I looked directly at Jake. "He killed Pastor Brown in such a manner that he would bleed out slowly. He was there in the forest watching. He took pleasure in knowing Pastor Brown's life was slowly fading from his body."

"That's sick," Dani said.

"It is," I agreed. "And while he was sorry Vinnie had stumbled onto the murder scene, it gave him pleasure to watch me and Landon find the body. Our arrival was an added bonus to him, and our horror brought him satisfaction. He watched us in those first moments and then, satisfied with what he had done, he left."

Jake sat forward in his chair. "Did you see anything other than connecting with his thoughts? Height? Weight? Hair color? Anything?"

I shook my head. "No. I'm sorry. I'm not sure why I picked up on him at all. He wasn't a victim. He wasn't the one I was to save. He really shouldn't even have been rattling around in my head."

"You linked to Pastor Brown, and Pastor Brown was linked to his killer in some way," Dani said. "Maybe you picked up an echo."

"Maybe. I guess that would make sense, but the last thing I want are the thoughts of a vicious killer taking up residence in my mind."

******

I was mentally and emotionally exhausted by the time Yukon and I arrived at the little backwoods cabin where I lived with seven dogs, four cats, eight rabbits, and a blind mule named Homer. The first thing I did when entering through the front door was pick up Moose and hold him tightly to my chest. I buried my face in his thick fur and felt the weight of the day begin to melt away. Moose let me take comfort in his presence for about thirty seconds before he began struggling to get down.

After experiencing the death of my sister, I was a physical and emotional wreck. I'm afraid I went just a bit off the deep end. Jake, who had been married to

Val and had taken over as my guardian, tried to help me, as did everyone else in my life, but there was no comfort in the world that would undo the horror I'd experienced. And then I met Moose, a large Maine coon who wandered into Jake's bar, where I worked and lived at the time. The minute I picked up the cantankerous cat and held him to my heart, the trauma I'd been experiencing somehow melted away. I won't go so far as to say Moose has magical powers—at least not any more than I do—but channeling people in life-and-death situations is more draining than I can tolerate, and the only one who can keep me grounded is a fuzzy coon with a cranky disposition.

    I gave Moose one last squeeze, then set him down. While all I really wanted to do was pour myself a glass of wine, take a hot bath, and wash away the dirtiness I felt when I stopped to remember that the killer had not only been watching me but had taken joy in my horror, six of the seven dogs needed to be exercised and all the animals needed to be fed. Luckily, I didn't have to deal with the long hours of darkness that enveloped us in the winter, so I fed the cats, then picked up my rifle and called all the dogs to follow me out into the sunny summer evening.

    Despite the fact that Yukon had already had quite a bit of exercise that day, he was still a puppy and, as such, had a lot of energy. Once I released the dogs to wander at will, he ran on ahead with Denali, my very protective wolf hybrid, and Shia, a husky pup who never seemed to get enough exercise no matter how often I took her out. Kodi and Juno, two Malamutes I'd adopted after their owner passed away, took up a position in the middle, while I followed with my three-legged dog Lucky and a mama retriever I'd adopted the previous Christmas, Honey.

Normally, I enjoyed walking with my family of canines, but today I couldn't quite shake the feeling of being watched. Of course, Denali, who would have sensed an intruder, was trotting happily along with nary a care in the world except for the rabbit that had darted into a nearby shrub, so I figured my feeling of being watched was most likely all in my mind. I willed myself to relax and enjoy my ever-growing family.

Most would consider seven dogs, four cats, eight rabbits, and a blind mule an excessive number of pets for one woman living in a very small cabin, but until recently, the town of Rescue hadn't had an animal shelter to house the strays that found their way onto the streets each year. My only choice when I happened upon an animal in need of saving was to bring them home. I was happy to share what I had with the animals who wandered in and out of my life. But now, thanks to Harley Medford, an action flick superstar, local town hero, and all-around great guy, we'd opened a shelter with limited hours of service this past spring. My goal, and that of the entire committee, was to run a full-service shelter with twenty-four-hour staffing, but as with all ambitious projects, sometimes the best you could do was the best you could do for the time being. Still, it hadn't been all that long ago that a shelter of any type had looked to be nothing more than a pipe dream.

"I should call Harley when I get home," I said to Lucky and Honey as we ambled along. "I think the movie he's been working on should be wrapping up soon. I'll be happy to have him back in Rescue for a while."

Honey barked once, as if agreeing with me. Harley was an actor in very high demand who spent most of his time either on location or at his home in Los Angeles, but he'd recently bought a home in Rescue where he intended to spend at least part of his time. At least that had been his plan when he bought it. In reality, he'd only managed to spend a few weekends in his new home since the previous December.

As we neared the edge of my property, I paused. Denali could probably use a longer walk, but I still had dogs to feed and the mule and rabbits to see to. I was about to call the dogs back when both Lucky and Honey, who stood close to my side, began to growl. I lifted my rifle and looked around. It wasn't uncommon to come across a predator, especially at this time of year. I called Kodi, Juno, Denali, Shia, and Yukon back to my side. All returned promptly except Denali. I was about to call for him specifically when I heard a rash of angry barking.

"Denali, come," I yelled at the top of my lungs before looking down at the other six dogs, who had nestled in tightly to surround me. I heard a yelp and then more barking. I instructed the six dogs to stay, then ran forward without stopping to consider the wisdom of doing so. I could hear a rustling in the brush ahead of me, which only caused me to run faster. I looked down to find Yukon running next to me. Without missing a step, I said, "I told you to stay." Yukon ignored me, remaining glued to my side as I ran toward the sound of Denali's angry growls. When I arrived at the edge of the heavily wooded area that served as a border for my property, I found him standing completely still while continuing to bark at something he sensed but I couldn't see. His shoulder was bleeding, but he didn't appear to be in any sort of mortal danger.

"Denali, come," I called again.

Denali turned and looked at me. He barked five more times in rapid succession, then turned and limped toward me. I fell to my knees to assess the extent of his injury. He had a deep gash in one shoulder, but otherwise he seemed fine. I threw my arms around his neck and wept with relief. "You're in so much trouble for not coming when I called you," I scolded as I hugged him tighter. Denali whined, so I pulled back a bit. I put my hand on his shoulder. "It's not too bad." I turned and looked at Yukon, who was sitting next to us, yet continued to growl as well. One thing was for sure: my very protective bodyguards weren't happy about whatever it was I couldn't see. I tried to tell myself it was nothing, perhaps a wolf or a bear. Then I remembered the presence I'd felt by the lake earlier in the day and felt a chill run down my spine.

I got up and walked slowly back to the cabin. Fortunately, Denali didn't seem to be hurt badly. I'd take a closer look when we got home. If the injury warranted it, I'd call Kelly Austin, the local veterinarian, and ask if I could get him in for a quick look, but based on what I could see, the injury would probably be fine with a good cleaning.

When we arrived at the spot where I'd told the dogs to stay, the rest of them were still waiting obediently. I greeted them by name, offering each a cuddle for a job well done, then headed back to the cabin.

Inside, I took a look at Denali's shoulder. On closer examination, I realized the wound had most likely been caused by a sharp branch as Denali ran toward whomever or whatever he'd intended to run off. I cleaned the cut, which had already stopped bleeding, then called Kelly, who offered to stop by for a quick look on her way home from the veterinary hospital. After I hung up, I fed all seven dogs. Juno and Kodi, who lived in the barn by choice, followed me out when I went to feed Homer and the rabbits. I'd tried to acclimate the huskies to the house when I'd first adopted them, but they'd been working dogs who had lived in a barn with their pack all their lives and preferred being outside to being cooped up inside.

"Hey, Homer," I said as I approached his stall. He couldn't see me, but he did seem to enjoy it when I spoke to him. "Sorry I'm late. The kids and I had a bit of excitement while out on our walk. Nearly scared the beejeebies out of me." I petted Homer on the face after I let myself into his stall. "Everyone is fine, though." I began shucking out the soiled hay. "Yukon broke command when I told him to stay. Honestly, I'm not sure what to do about that." I walked into a nearby stall to grab fresh hay to spread around. "On one hand, part of being a good S-and-R dog is to obey the instructions of your handler no matter what. The dog's life as well as the lives of the people involved could very well depend on it." I scattered the fresh hay around Homer's stall, being sure to leave a thick layer of hay along the back, where he liked to sleep. "On the other, he's still a pup, and I know he sensed I was in danger. I guess part of me is happy he felt the need to protect me." I stood back and admired my handiwork, then headed to the bin where I stored Homer's oats and veggies. "I guess I'll talk to Jake about it to see what he suggests. The last thing I want to do is quell the natural instincts I identified as markers for being a good S-and-R dog in the first place."

I finished tucking Homer in and moved on to the rabbits. I spoke to them as I cleaned their cage and fed them, then said a final good night to Kodi and Juno, picked up the rifle I'd leaned against the wall near the door, and went back to the cabin.

Kelly was pulling up in the drive when I came out. I didn't know what I would do without the generous doctor, who not only was willing to make house calls for minor scrapes and scratches but extended me a 90 percent discount when I did have cause to bring one of my animals in for more serious illnesses and injuries.

"Thank you so much for coming by." I hugged the woman I also considered to be a friend. "Initially, I believed the scratch to be deeper than it actually is. Once I got it cleaned up, it didn't look too bad. Still, better safe than sorry."

"It's not a problem at all. I'm always happy to check in on your menagerie."

Denali loved Kelly and stood quietly while she checked the gash in his shoulder. She cleaned it out with a special wash and applied an ointment. "I don't think he'll bother the injury based on where it is, so we may be able to avoid the cone of shame," Kelly said. "But keep an eye on it. I'll leave the wash and ointment. Clean it with the wash and apply the ointment twice a day until they're gone. If the injury becomes red or pussy, bring him in right away."

"Okay. Thanks."

Kelly stood up from the kneeling position she'd taken to treat the wound. "Like I said, it's not a problem. I stopped by the shelter today to look at that husky that was brought in last week. The antibiotics I prescribed don't seem to be knocking out the infection in his abdomen the way I hoped. I think I'll need to do surgery to clean everything out. I can do it tomorrow. Justine said she'd stop by to pick him up on her way in." Justine was Kelly's assistant and also served as a shelter volunteer.

"Okay. That should be fine."

Kelly left, and I hunted around the kitchen for something to make for dinner. I hadn't been to the market in weeks, so the pickings were slim. Settling on a can of soup, I emptied it into a bowl, then placed it in the microwave. It had been a long day and the glass of wine and hot bath I'd planned for later were looking better and better. Of course, I first had to clean cat boxes and answer the voicemails that had been left on my cell while Kelly had been here.

Once the soup was hot, I settled in at my small dining table and listened to the first message.

"Hey, Harm, it's Chloe. There's a rumor going around that you went out on a rescue today and found a body. Call me."

Chloe Rivers was my best friend, and I tended to share most of my life's secrets with her, but I wasn't sure if I was supposed to talk about Pastor Brown's death yet. Officer Houston had asked the team not to say anything until they completed their initial investigation and contacted next of kin. Knowing

Chloe, she wouldn't let it go until I told her the entire story, so I decided to ignore the call and hope she would let it go until tomorrow.

I took a slurp of my soup, then listened to the second message.

"Harmony, it's Harley. I'm sorry I missed you. I had a few minutes before I needed to head out for the evening, so I thought I'd call to say hi. I won't be able to call you back; my agent wants me to attend a party that will probably drag on until the wee hours of the morning. I finished the film and hope to be home in a week or two. I'll try calling you tomorrow if I can find a spare minute."

Dang. I really wanted to talk to Harley. I was sorry I'd missed his call. We'd become friends when he'd come back to Rescue the previous December to track down the man who'd killed his high school friend. Before that, I hadn't seen him since his family moved away when he was a senior in high school. I'll admit I'd been crushing on Harley ever since I could remember, but after he'd left Alaska, he'd become an international film star, which meant he was completely unobtainable no matter how nice and generous he'd turned out to be in my book. Glancing down at my unfinished bowl of soup, I realized it was time to move on to the wine-and-bath portion of the evening.

******

Despite the bath, the wine, and my fatigue, sleep didn't come easily. There were voices in my head, visions trying to find their way into reality, images I wasn't yet willing to deal with. I closed my eyes tight, tossing and turning for what seemed like hours before finally slipping into a restless slumber.

The windowless room was dark and heavy with scents too overwhelming to process. The air was stale, the ground cold, hard, and unforgiving. The woman faded in and out of consciousness as terror strangled her with fear, pain, and hopelessness. The rough ropes cut into her wrists and thick tape covered her mouth. How long had she been here? How much longer could she survive? And did she even want to? She wanted to live, yes, but she knew that in death would come the peace she longed for.

I screamed, flailing my arms against an unseen captor as I struggled myself awake. I was bathed in sweat, the bedclothes twisted and tangled around my body. I gasped for fresh air and I felt my lungs expand with the oxygen they'd previously been denied. I threw my blankets to the floor as if they were the enemy and then sat straight up as I struggled to overcome the fear that threatened to destroy me. Moose jumped onto my bed and burrowed his way into my lap, and all five house dogs ran around, barking fiercely at the unseen intruder that had caused their human so much distress.

"It's okay," I said, hugging Moose to my chest and gasping for more air. "It's okay," I said again. Honey jumped onto the bed and burrowed her head under my arm, while Yukon, Denali, and Shia took defensive positions between the bed and the bedroom door with guttural growls and teeth bared.

I took several more breaths. Slow, deep inhalations that chased the remainder of the nightmare from my mind. "It's okay," I said again, in as calm a voice as I could muster. Lucky was sitting next to the bed with his head resting on the mattress, while Honey climbed into my lap the minute Moose decided his job was done and jumped from the bed to the floor.

"It was just a dream," I assured the animals as I clicked on the bedside lamp. "Just a dream," I repeated, as if to convince myself.

I rolled my legs to the side of the bed and sat there for a moment while my heart rate slowed. Then I stood up. The room looked wrong somehow, but I couldn't put my finger on what it was. I supposed a nightmare as severe as the one I'd just had would leave a bit of confusion in its wake.

I helped Lucky up onto the bed, then called the others up as well. Surrounded by five very concerned canines, I let them offer comfort as I chased away the last of the dream.

After Val died, I'd had nightmares all the time. Explicit, gut-wrenching nightmares that had me living through Val's death over and over again. The dreams had been so real, seeming more like visions than dreams, but with time and the love and patience of Jake and everyone else on the team, they had become less frequent and less intense.

Tonight's nightmare was just as intense as those, yet different. It wasn't Val in the dark, damp room, and it wasn't me. It was someone I didn't know but had connected with. Was that even possible? I'd been connecting with people in need of help for years, but always when I was conscious and knew with a certainty that the images in my head were real, not dreams.

Once the dogs had settled down, I got up and pulled on a robe. The dogs followed me as I wandered into the kitchen. I took a glass from the cupboard and poured myself a glass of water. If there was one thing you could say about the water in Rescue, it was as pure and cold as you were apt to find anywhere.

After drinking the entire glass, I used a hand to wipe my damp hair from my face. It had been years since I'd wakened in a cold sweat. Sure, I had nightmares when a strong storm blew through, but my dream this evening had felt real, raw, and uncensored.

Wandering back into the bedroom, I stripped the bed. Then I found new sheets in the linen closet and layered the blankets atop them. I grabbed fresh pajamas, then went into the bathroom for a long, hot shower. I wanted to numb my mind. To push away the images I'd seen, though the feeling of absolute horror I'd just experienced wasn't likely to let go any time soon.

After I'd showered, I combed and braided my long hair, pulled a heavy robe over my pj's, then padded into the living room, where I tossed a log on the fire. Curling up on the sofa, I snuggled with my pack of dogs, watching the flames rise and fall as the wood slowly burned from log to ash.

I thought about calling Jake, but it was two in the morning and I hated to wake him. Besides, he'd just worry about my mental health and might even suspend me from active rescues if he felt I was beginning to slip into the delirium that had become my refuge in those first days after Val's death. No, it was better, I decided, to power through the night on my own. Things would look better in the daylight, and fortunately in northern Alaska, there was a lot of that at this time of the year.

I thought about having another glass of wine but settled for milk. I searched around for the remote and clicked on the television to provide some company and background noise. The dogs all curled up either on the sofa with me or in front of it. The demons who lived in my dreams couldn't find me as long as I was awake, so I settled in to wait out the darkness, which was only about a half an hour away.

Chapter 3

Tuesday, June 19

I woke the next morning to abundant sunshine streaming through the large picture window at the front of the cabin. It was early yet, barely six, so I figured I had plenty of time to take the dogs for a long walk before going into town for my shift at the animal shelter. I tried to slip from the sofa, but Honey was sleeping on my legs, Shia was on top of my feet, and Yukon was laying on my right arm. It was a good thing I had an extra-wide sofa, which took up most of the room. I'd chosen this one specifically because I loved to cuddle with my animals on dark, snowy days and wanted to have room for everyone who wanted to join in.

"Hey, guys," I said as I tried to wiggle free. "It's time to be up and at 'em."

Yukon popped up, all wriggling body and wagging tail, while Honey simply yawned and looked at me with one eye open and one still closed. Lucky, who slept in a dog bed next to the sofa, thumped his tail once, then went back to sleep. I looked around the room for Denali, but he was nowhere in sight. He'd seemed skittish after our adventure the previous day, and even more skittish since my meltdown last night. Poor guy. It must be hard to be tasked with trying to protect a crazy woman.

Once I was finally able to untangle myself from my canine bedfellows, I slipped a heavy sweatshirt over my head and headed into the kitchen. I started the coffeemaker, then went to the back of the house, where I found Denali looking intently out the window. "What are you looking at?"

He turned and greeted me with a wagging tail but cautious eyes. I scratched my hands through his hair before going back into the kitchen to pour my first cup of coffee of the day. By the time I'd finished my second, my lazy dogs were up, so I dressed in warm clothes against the morning chill and started out into the lush spring morning. Yukon and Shia took the lead, as they usually did, Juno and Kodi fell into the middle, and Lucky and Honey stayed glued to my side. What was unusual today was that Denali, who normally liked to be the leader of the pack, hung back with Lucky, Honey, and me. My first thought was that he was still spooked by my nightmare. My second, and probably the more accurate of the two, was that he sensed something none of the other dogs were able to. If I had to guess, the something he sensed was something I'd just as soon not share my little corner of paradise with.

After all seven dogs seemed to have met their exercise needs, we headed back to the cabin. It took me an hour every morning to feed everyone and make sure they were set for the day, but most times, the time spent with my menagerie was the best hour of my day. There were people who thought I was some sort of a hero for saving the animals I had, but truth be told, the animals had saved me. Without them to love and focus my energy on, I'd most likely have gone plumb crazy years ago.

The animals seen to, I showered and dressed for the day. While it was cool this morning, the afternoon temps were predicted to be quite mild, so I decided to go with layers I could peel off as the day wore on. After a perfunctory search of my kitchen cabinets, which hadn't magically been filled by the grocery fairy while I slumbered, I grabbed a sleeve of crackers, then set out for my trip into town. By the time I arrived at the shelter it was after nine. I took a minute to admire the work the volunteers had been able to accomplish in such a short amount of time, then went to the room in the back we were currently using as an office. "What do we have here?" I asked Serena Walters, one of our regulars,

"Oh good, you're here. I was just about to call you. Some guy who was passing through dropped off this baby moose. He's really cute, but he doesn't look good. I have no idea what to do with him."

I knelt and looked at the tiny thing that couldn't be more than a few days old. "He's so small. He must have been a twin." Calves were usually around thirty pounds at birth, but twins tended to be half as large.

"The guy said he was driving along the highway and pulled over to take a call. He got out of his car and heard a wailing that sounded like a puppy, or maybe a baby, coming from a drainage ditch and went to investigate. He saw this little one lying there. He looked around, but the mother was nowhere in sight. It appears the baby may have broken his leg." Serena looked up at me with a slight expression of panic. "I know you've talked about expanding to include wild animal rescue, but there's no way we're ready for it now."

"Yeah, there's no way we can take care of a newborn with the staff we have. Especially a newborn with an injury. I'll take him to Kelly and see what she suggests. If need be, I have an extra stall in my barn. I think Homer would enjoy a roommate, at least temporarily."

I called Kelly to give her a heads-up about what I was bringing in. She assured me that she'd instruct her receptionist to get me into a room as soon as I arrived. I wrapped the baby in a blanket and picked him up, estimating, as I'd thought, that he weighed around fifteen pounds. The fact that he wasn't at all active concerned me more than just a little bit. I wondered how long he'd been abandoned. Not long, I assumed. Baby moose were completely helpless. If he'd been on his own long, he'd most likely have succumbed to a predator with a few hours.

When we arrived at the veterinary hospital, I was shown directly into an exam room. I set the moose, still wrapped in the blanket, on the exam table, speaking to him softly while we waited for Kelly. Thankfully, we didn't have to wait long.

"Poor little guy," Kelly said as she ran her hands over the mostly limp body, taking care with the injured leg.

"Is it broken?" I asked.

"Yeah, it's broken," Kelly said. "I'll need to set it and then try to get some nourishment into him. I have a milk supplement that should work okay." She frowned as she ran her hands over the baby's abdomen. "He's in pretty bad shape. I'm not holding out a lot of hope, but I'm willing to do what I can. If he makes it through the next twenty-four hours, he might have a shot."

"What can I do?" I asked, my throat clogged with emotion. Those of us who made our homes in Alaska understood the harsh environment we had to deal with. Every year the area's wildlife gave birth, and every year a good percentage of that newborn wildlife died. It was the circle of life, which dictated that sick or injured newborns became food for the carnivores who depended on fresh meat to feed their own young. The fact that life was so fragile wasn't something I liked to think about, but I accepted it as true. But fate had delivered this calf into my arms, and if it was in my power, I'd help him to be one of the survivors who made it into adulthood.

"If I can get him stabilized, do you have somewhere he can bunk until the leg heals?" Kelly asked as she started an IV.

"There's an extra stall in my barn. And I have a space heater, so it's warm. He can stay there as long as he needs. If the leg heals and he survives his rough start in the world, maybe we can set him free in the fall. Or if that's too soon, maybe next spring."

I couldn't help but notice the look of doubt that crept into Kelly's eyes. "Maybe. The leg may be problematic; it's too soon to know for sure. If releasing him into the wild isn't an option, I know a refuge that might take him. For now, let's focus on getting him stabilized. I'd like to keep him here for a few days. If he makes it through then, we'll talk about a long-term plan."

Kelly and I spoke for a while longer, then I left to go back to the shelter. I was glad she'd agreed to do what she could, but the truth of the matter was, if the baby moose was going to be in the hospital for several days I was going to need to sell my cabin to pay the veterinary bill. Of course, Kelly had always given me a huge discount and allowed me to make payments when it came to treatments for the strays I collected on a regular basis, so I hoped she'd work something out with me this time too.

"How is he?" Serena asked the moment I walked through the front door of the shelter.

"I'm not sure yet. He's in bad shape, but Kelly's going to do what she can. If she can get him stabilized, I guess he'll come stay in my barn for the short term. After that, we'll have to see."

"Poor little guy." Serena had a look of sympathy on her face. "The gang and I are pulling for him. Just let us know if there's anything we can do."

I smiled. "I will." The volunteers who donated a good portion of their free time to staff the shelter were some of the best people you were likely to find anywhere. I considered myself very fortunate to have them as friends.

"Did Kelly say how the husky Justine picked up for surgery was doing?" Serena asked as I hung up my jacket.

"I didn't think to ask, but I'm sure the surgery went well or she would have said something. I'll call over later to check on them."

Serena handed me a cup of coffee. "Seems like things are getting busy for us even though we're just getting started."

"Yes," I agreed as I took a sip, then set the mug on the desk. "Yes, they are." I picked up a stack of mail and thumbed through it. "By the way, whatever happened with the Lab that was brought in a few days ago?"

"We tracked down his owner. Apparently, he was left out in the yard during that last big storm. The owner had no idea part of his fence had blown down and the dog got out. The guy said he'd been looking for him for days. He seemed really glad to have him back."

I frowned. "I wonder why he didn't check with us right away when he realized his dog was missing."

"He said he didn't even know we were open. I guess we haven't done enough to announce ourselves, given the fact that Rescue has never had a shelter before. Folks aren't used to checking in with us."

Serena had a point. We'd wanted to have a soft opening, accepting only a few animals until we were able to sign up enough volunteers to take care of the place seven days a week. We still hoped to be able to hire staff at some point, and the outdoor runs were far from completed, but we ought to be open enough to let the town know we were ready to house the strays that roamed the streets of Rescue every summer.

"We should have a grand opening," I said as I set down the stack of envelopes. "Let folks know we're open for business."

"Maybe we can make it a fund-raiser. The vet bills are piling up fast, even with the huge discount Kelly gives us."

"That's a good idea," I answered. "The only way this place is going to make it in the long run is if we can rally the community around it. We may as well get started on building that allegiance."

"When should we do it?" Serena asked.

I paused to consider her question. "It'd be nice if Harley could be here; none of this would be possible if not for his donation. I think he's supposed to be back in town within the next few weeks. I missed a call from him last night, but he said he'd try to call me back today. If he does, I'll try to get his schedule. Then we can take it from there."

"Maybe we can use some of his movie-star status to get folks from out of town to come. We really should have a reserve to draw from for emergencies, and it would be totally awesome to hire full-time staff to oversee daily operations."

I nodded as Serena and I went to work cleaning the cages of the handful of dogs we currently housed. "Maybe Harley will have some ideas about soliciting money from large donors and corporate sponsors, which is what we really need to do that. And there are grants out there we can revisit now that we have a facility."

"I have a cousin who works for the *Los Angeles Times*. Maybe I can talk to her about doing a human-interest story about our shelter. Normally, it wouldn't be her thing, but when you consider that Harley Medford is involved, it might just fly."

"And maybe I'll set up a website and a Facebook page too. The more presence we have, the more likely we are to come up with the money we need to do everything we want to do."

Serena and I had just finished with the last cage and were going back to the office when Chloe came charging in. I frowned when I realized she didn't look happy. "I called and left you a message last night," she accused me before I could even say hello.

I cringed. "I know. I'm sorry I didn't call you back. I didn't see the message until late, so I decided to wait until today to return the call, and then I guess I forgot."

"I can't believe you didn't call to tell me about Pastor Brown the minute you knew." Chloe's cheeks were red with anger. "I'm your best friend. You should want to tell me everything, and yet I had to find out about the biggest news to hit town in forever from Raelene Cole."

"What's wrong with Pastor Brown?" Serena asked.

"He's dead," I answered a bit too abruptly. I loved Chloe, but I wasn't in the mood to handle one of her meltdowns. I took a deep breath to calm myself and looked at Chloe with what I hoped was a sincere expression of apology. "And I'm sorry I didn't call you. Officer Houston wanted to keep a lid on things until he had the opportunity to poke around a bit and notify the next of kin. Still, I should have told you what was going on."

"Darn right you should have. You know I can keep a secret."

"I know. I'm sorry."

"Enough with the apologies," Serena said in a tone a bit too loud not to hint at a certain level of hysteria. "Pastor Brown is dead?"

I nodded. Raelene Cole was the biggest gossip in town. If she knew what had happened, it wouldn't be long before everyone else knew too, so I may as well fill Serena in. "Pastor Brown's body was found near Glacier Lake yesterday. We found him while we were out looking for a missing child. He'd been murdered."

"What do you mean, murdered?" Serena asked as her face drained of all color. "Who would murder him?"

I briefly explained what I knew, which wasn't a lot, but was more than Raelene did, which placated Chloe somewhat but almost sent Serena over the edge.

"Wow," Serena said as she slid to the floor. "I'm having a hard time dealing with this."

"Did you know Pastor Brown well?" I asked as I beat myself up for not handling the situation with a bit more sensitivity and decorum.

Serena nodded, then put her head down. "He was my pastor. I've been going to his church since I was a child. My family just had him to dinner two weeks ago. Oh God."

I knelt and placed my hands on Serena's shoulders. I stood slowly, helping her to her feet, then to a chair. Chloe, who seemed to be over her snit, brought Serena a glass of water."

"I'm sorry," I said for the third time as I sat down across from Serena.

"Me too," Chloe said. "Here I was, carrying on like a raving lunatic about not hearing the news first. I didn't even stop to think how this would affect the folks who really knew him."

Serena took a sip of her water. "It's okay. I know you don't attend his church. You couldn't have known."

"Maybe not, but I should have been a lot more sensitive. Hearing the news from Raelene made me angry, but it also freaked me out. I guess it was easier to go with the anger."

Serena looked up at me, tears streaming down her face. "I just don't understand any of this. The cold-blooded murder of a sweet man like Pastor Brown is something I'd expect to happen in a big city with lots of crime, not here in Rescue, where most folks don't even bother to lock their doors."

"I know." I agreed. "It was a shock to us all."

"Are there any leads?" Chloe asked.

"I don't know," I answered honestly. "I haven't spoken to Officer Houston since shortly after the body was found. I'm sure once the police know what's going on, they'll issue a statement of some sort to the newspaper."

Naturally, I was curious about what was going on with the investigation as well, but I doubted Houston would tell me even if I asked. Maybe he'd talk to Jake. He was, after all, the head of the search-and-rescue team, and it seemed Houston would want to maintain a close working relationship him. I had a shift at Neverland later in the day, so maybe I'd ask Jake to nose around a bit while I was there.

"I should call my parents," Serena said. "They're going to take it hard. Particularly my mother. I can't believe the pastor is dead. I just saw him on Sunday and nothing seemed wrong."

"I don't suppose you happen to know what he planned to do after Sunday services?" I asked.

"Not specifically. His usual routine is to have lunch with one of the families who attend the church. He's good about spreading himself around, making sure everyone who wants to have him to their home has the opportunity. Our family has hosted him three times this year, the most recent two weeks ago."

"And how did he seem when you saw him on Sunday?" I asked.

"Seem?"

"Did he seem distracted or nervous? Perhaps he was more preoccupied than usual, or maybe he didn't smile as much as he usually did."

Serena shook her head. "He didn't seem different at all. His sermon was about forgiveness. It touched on the concept of not just forgiving others but forgiving yourself for something you may have done in the past that you felt deep remorse for. It was very moving, and I got a lot out of it."

"I wonder if there's a way to know who Pastor Brown had dinner with on Sunday," I said.

"His secretary would probably know, although now that I think about it, I'm almost certain Jolene Pinewood mentioned he was going to be dining with her family. Is it important?"

"It might come in handy to know where Pastor Brown was last seen alive," I answered.

Serena took a deep breath. "Okay. I'll call Jolene. If Pastor Brown did dine at her house on Sunday, is there anything specific you want me to ask her?"

"Just ask her whether he seemed to be stressed or worried about anything. And find out what time he left and if he mentioned where he was going next."

I spoke with Chloe while Serena left the room to make her call. I could see how difficult this was for her, but I was sure it was important for her to do what she could to help. Action, I'd learned through my own life, was the best way to deal with grief that was too large to bear.

After a few minutes, Serena returned. "That was rough. Jolene hadn't heard about Pastor Brown, so I had to explain things. The poor thing is really upset." A tear slid down Serena's cheek. "We all are."

I waited in silence for her to continue. I didn't know Pastor Brown well, but I was sure that for his flock and friends, this was devastating.

"The pastor did dine with Jolene's family on Sunday. He came over right after the service let out, which was around one o'clock, and stayed until around four. Jolene invited him to stay and watch a movie with them, but he declined, mentioning he'd arranged to meet with a man who used to live in Rescue a long time ago and was back for a visit that evening."

"Did Jolene know what the man's name was or where they were meeting?" I asked.

"Pastor Brown didn't say. Jolene told me that while he didn't seem stressed exactly, there was something—a hesitation in his voice—when he mentioned the man, as if he wasn't entirely thrilled to be meeting with him but at the same time seemed curious about why he wanted to see him."

"It seems Jolene picked up quite a lot about the meeting and Pastor Brown's feelings about it, considering the pastor didn't really say much."

"You know how Jolene is," Serena replied. "She's really sensitive and very good about picking up subtle clues. I suppose being observant served her well when she was a social worker."

"Yeah, I remember hearing she was good at her job. I wonder if she picked up any other clues that might help us figure out what happened."

"If you think she might be able to tell you more, you can call her later, after she calms down a bit."

"Thank you. I might do that. For now, why don't you go home to be with your family?" I suggested. "I'll stay here until the next volunteer arrives."

"Thanks. I think I'll do that. I want to be the one to tell Mom before she hears it from a neighbor." Serena went into the bathroom to wash her face, then headed home.

"I guess I never stopped to think how folks were going to react to the news," I said to Chloe. "I mean, I knew it would be a shock to the community, but it sounds like Pastor Brown was an important friend to a lot of people."

"Yeah. I feel like an idiot. I knew who he was, but I didn't really know him. Still, I shouldn't have reacted the way I did. It was thoughtless and insensitive and completely childish." Chloe sat down next to me and put her head on my shoulder. She took my hand in hers in a gesture of apology. "I just can't imagine who would do something like this. It must have been someone passing through. Surely no one who lives here would be capable of such a brutal act."

I sat up straighter and looked at Chloe. "The person who killed Pastor Brown may very well have been a transient passing through, or it might have been the former town resident he was meeting, but it could just as likely have been someone who lives here in town. Someone we come into contact with every day. You never know what's going on behind closed doors. I want you to be careful. Lock up when you're home alone, and make sure you leave the restaurant with your staff in the evening. I don't want you to be alone. Ever."

Chloe narrowed her gaze. "You're scaring me."

"I'm not trying to scare you, I'm just warning you to be careful until whoever did this is caught."

Chloe opened her mouth, I was sure to argue, when my phone buzzed. "Dang it," I said.

"What is it?" Chloe asked.

"It's Jake. I've been called out for a rescue. He wants me to stop by my place to pick up Yukon." I looked around the office. "I told Serena I'd stay here until the next volunteer arrived."

"I can stay," Chloe offered.

"I don't want you to be alone."

Chloe looked at the staffing chart. "It looks like the next volunteer is Anne. She's the only one scheduled this afternoon. Are you trying to say it will be okay for her to be alone but not me?"

I shook my head. "No, I guess not."

Chloe put her hands on her hips. "You're freaked out and overreacting. There's no reason to think the person who killed Pastor Brown would have any interest whatsoever in me, or anyone else for that matter. In most murders, the killer turns out to have a personal agenda."

I let out a breath. "You're right. I'm being ridiculous. I'm sure none of us are in danger."

Chloe hugged me. "I do appreciate your concern, but I'll be fine."

"I know you need to get back to the restaurant, so if you have to go before Anne gets here, it's fine. I'll give you the numbers of a couple of the guys who plan to come by this evening to see if they can come in early. That way Anne won't have to be alone." I grabbed my backpack, which I'd left hanging on a hook. Most of the gear I'd need for the rescue was in my Jeep, and it wouldn't take long to grab Yukon and meet Jake and the others at Neverland. "Jake didn't provide any details about who's missing or where they were last seen, but if it turns out to be a quick and easy rescue, I'll come back when we're done."

"Harm," Chloe said as I hurried toward the exterior door.

"Yeah?"

"Be careful. Despite what I just said about none of us being in danger, I have a bad feeling about things."

"I know. Me too," I agreed before I headed out to my Jeep. As hard as I tried, I couldn't get the woman from my dreams out of my mind.

Chapter 4

It turned out the search-and-rescue request had come from Officer Houston, who'd been contacted by Nolan White to find his wife, Silvia. She was sixty-two and had lived in Rescue for as long as I could remember. She'd been a doctor, serving the community for decades before she retired this past winter. According to Nolan, Silvia had gone to her yoga class at around eight o'clock that morning. She'd called him a short time later to let him know she'd made plans to have breakfast with an old acquaintance and would be home well before noon, when they were driving to Fairbanks for a movie. When she hadn't gotten home by one, Nolan began calling her friends, who said Silvia had left yoga at about nine-fifteen with a middle-aged man driving a dark blue Ford Focus. The man had brown hair cut short and was wearing a dark-colored, long-sleeved shirt.

"Okay, I think I understand the situation, but I'm not sure where I come in," I said to Jake, who was sitting alone in the bar with Officer Houston. "While this is a missing persons case, and we do quite often look for missing persons, it isn't like we have an area to search. It sounds like Silvia left by car with a man she knew. She could be anywhere, and we don't know for certain that she's in any sort of trouble. I mean, she did take off with some guy. Maybe there's simply hanky-panky going on and she lost track of time."

"I agree," Jake said, "which is why I didn't call in the others. At least not yet. I did speak to Jordan, and she said Silvia isn't at all the sort to either cheat on her husband or to forget about time and worry everyone. We wouldn't normally put much stock in a report from a husband saying his wife is an hour late getting home, but after what happened with Pastor Brown, we didn't want to brush it off either. If Silvia is in trouble, I hoped you might be able to make a connection. I know it's a long shot, but it seemed like one worth exploring."

I glanced at the town's newest police chief. I thought he was probably a few years older than Jake, handsome in a rugged sort of way. He had thick hair he wore short, dark eyes that didn't show much emotion, a firm jaw, and a scar that ran from the outer corner of his left eye, across his forehead, and close to his hair line. He'd been in town about a month, and while I'd certainly noticed him, and even worked with him, I'd never talked to him outside my place on the S&R team. Our team had participated in several rescues since he'd come to town, including the search for Vinnie yesterday, so I suspected he had an inkling of my unique gift, but we hadn't worked closely enough together for me to be sure what he thought about it.

"Okay," I said. "If you both think this is a good idea, I'm willing to try." I took a deep breath, closed my eyes, and focused. I tried to see Silvia's face in my head as I let her name roll over and over in my mind. It took several minutes, but the longer I meditated, the more certain I was that I could feel something. "I sense fear. No, not fear, terror. It's dark, and Silvia is unable to move." I paused as I tried to come up with additional details. "I think her hands and legs are bound. I don't sense physical pain, but I feel a great degree of emotional distress."

"Can you see where Silvia is being held?" Jake asked.

I shook my head. "It's dark. Totally dark. And cold. I'm guessing she must be in a cave, or maybe some sort of an underground cellar. I get the feeling she doesn't know where she is." I concentrated harder. "I think she may have been knocked out and when she awoke, she found herself in a location totally devoid of light." I opened my eyes. "If she can't see where she is, or if she doesn't know, there's no way I can know." I looked at Houston. "I can only see what she sees and know what she knows. And even that's pretty random."

"Just tell us what you can," Houston responded in a deep and surprisingly gentle voice.

"Is she alone?" Jake asked. "Do you sense another person? Her captor, perhaps?"

I closed my eyes again. I had to fight the panic that wanted to bubble up from my core as I remembered my dream. I knew I hadn't been connecting with Silvia in the dream I had during the night. Silvia hadn't turned up missing until this morning. Still, there were eerie similarities. "I don't sense anyone else. Silvia's really scared. Her fear is so predominant in her mind that it's hard to pick up on anything else."

"If we're going to save her, we need more," Jake encouraged. "Is there anything at all that might tell us where to look?"

A flash of something went through my mind. "There's a sign. Not where she is now, but where she was before. I can't be certain it's from anywhere she even was today, but I sense she was looking at it or thinking of it when everything went black."

"What does the sign say?" Jake asked.

I focused harder. "It's a trailhead sign. One of the brown ones that are scattered around the area." I tried to bring the sign into focus, but Silvia had only glanced at it or thought of it for a heartbeat before everything went dark. I opened my eyes. "I can't read which trail the sign is marking. I think whoever Silvia was with brought her to the trailhead, then knocked her out and took her to the place she's being held."

"Can you pick up on anything she remembered before that?" Officer Houston asked.

"No. She was too scared. She wasn't thinking about the past, only the present. The sign was a brief flash in her mind, and she didn't hang on to the memory or image long enough to place it in context. Signs like the one I sensed are all over the place, but…" I paused. "This one was damaged. A corner was missing." I looked at Jake. "The lost mine trailhead."

Jake's eyes narrowed. "There are dozens of mines in the area."

"Call in the others." I said, and then I looked at Officer Houston. "Have one of your men go by Silvia's house. Have them get clothing from her husband. Items she's worn recently. Put them in plastic bags, then have as many men as you can round up meet us at the trailhead." I looked back to Jake. "If she's being held in one of the mines, we might not know where to look, but Yukon and Sitka should be able to pick up a scent."

Jake called Wyatt and had him call in the other team members. Officer Houston offered to go fetch Silvia's clothing himself, so Jake, Sitka, Yukon, and I could set off for the trailhead. The parking area was deserted, seeming to indicate that if the person who'd abducted Silvia had driven her to this location, he or she was long gone by now.

Jake and I got out of his truck and looked around. We'd need to wait for the others, but it wasn't a bad thing to take a moment to get the lay of the land. The dogs were happily sniffing at everything in sight, but they didn't yet know who they were looking for.

I sat down on a log and tried to focus on Silvia while Jake called Wyatt for a status update.

"Anything?" Jake asked after a minute.

I shook my head. "I sense Silvia is alive, but I think she might be unconscious now. It isn't a restful state, like sleeping. She's struggling. And while I wasn't able to pick up any physical pain before, now that her mind has calmed a bit, I can sense physical distress. If Wyatt hasn't already thought of it, you should have Dani stand by for a medical extraction. Have Jordan standing by at the hospital as well."

"Wyatt is on it and the others are waiting for our call. Wyatt and Landon are on the way out with Officer Houston. He has the clothing we requested. I'm not sure how many backups Houston was able to track down, but we'll find out when he gets here."

"What do you think about Officer Houston?" I asked in an offhand manner.

"I like him. He worked for Boston PD for ten years and, from what I can tell, was a highly regarded officer before making detective two years ago. When the opening for chief came up in Rescue this past May, he applied for and got the job."

"Sounds overqualified. I'm sensing a story of some sort behind his move from Boston to Rescue."

"Probably, but he seems like a good guy and his story is his to tell or not."

I didn't disagree with Jake, but I found I was a lot more interested in the story behind the man than I probably should be. I was considering the wisdom of asking Landon to do a background search on him when the man in question pulled up with the two bags of clothes we'd been waiting for. By the time Jake and Houston had agreed on a strategy, Landon and Wyatt arrived as well. Given the terrain of the area, it was decided that four teams would search the area in a grid formation. I was to take grid one, with Yukon and Officer Houston. Landon was going to take grid two with two of Houston's men, Jake grid three with Sitka, and Wyatt grid four with Austin, who had called in just as the team was ready to roll out.

Each team had identical maps and two-way radios tuned to the same channel. We hiked over to our grid, gave Yukon the scent, and Houston and I prepared to follow.

"What happens if the dog picks up the scent and follows it into a different grid?" Houston asked.

"We'll follow. We start off sort of spread out so we can cover more territory, but once one or both dogs pick up a scent, we'll probably all end up in the same place. It's important to maintain constant radio contact so everyone has the same information."

"Have you been doing this long?" Houston asked, as Yukon led us off the trail and into dense forest that was steep and rocky and made walking difficult.

"Unofficially, since I was a teenager. My sister, Val, was married to Jake. She was a member of the S-and-R team, so I spent a lot of time hanging out in the bar manning the radio while the others were out. When I turned eighteen, Jake let me join officially."

"I wasn't aware Jake was married," Houston said as we slowed to climb over a rock formation.

"He's not anymore. Val died during a rescue when I was seventeen."

"I'm sorry. That must have been hard on you."

I told Yukon to wait and then took out my binoculars to scan the area. "It was," I said as I looked for a likely place for Silvia to have been stashed. "We're going to hit a natural cliff if we continue east," I said. "It doesn't appear Yukon has picked up Silvia's scent, so I suggest we double back to the spot where we took the left fork and try going in the other direction."

Houston shrugged. "You're the expert."

I used the radio to call Jake and let him know what we were doing. He informed me that Sitka had alerted twice since the beginning of the search. He seemed confused at first but finally headed upriver. He followed the scent for a while but seemed to lose it after a bit. He seemed to want to double back, but Jake was pretty sure Silvia and her captor had taken the river route at least for a while. I told him that we'd head in his direction, then signed off.

"We're going to change our search parameter," I informed Houston. I pulled out my map and laid it on a rock. "We're here." I pointed to a location. "Jake's team is about here." I pointed to a second spot. "Jake thinks Silvia and her captor would have taken the river route. We're going to head northeast. We should intersect them right about here."

"What is this here?" Houston pointed to a hilly place that wasn't all that far from the parking area.

"Low-lying mountains. Steep, but not particularly large. Easy to traverse in the summer, a bear in the winter."

"Would one be likely to find mines in this area?"

I frowned. "Yeah. I guess. There are old mines and natural caverns scattered all over this area. Generally, the higher the elevation, the more you're likely to find. Why do you ask?"

Houston took another moment to study the map. "It just seems to me that whoever kidnapped Silvia wouldn't have wanted to go on a long hike through the forest before stashing her somewhere. He wouldn't want his hiding place to be easily found, but he'd want it to be convenient should he plan to return at any point. We started our grid here." Houston pointed to the map. "Jake and Sitka started here. They had a scent early on, so they've been following the river trail. What if the captor parked here?" Houston indicated a spot north of the parking area and trailhead and below where Jake and Sitka entered the search. "If they came in here," Houston ran his finger along a dirt trail, "and hugged the river here," he continued to run his large finger across the surface of the map, "wouldn't it be possible for the kidnapper to double back and hike up the mountain here?"

"Yeah, I suppose, but why would he bother to head up the river in the first place if his destination was closer to the road?"

"To provide a scent for the dogs to follow leading away from the victim's actual location."

I had to hand it to the handsome officer. His theory made sense. "So Sitka picked up the scent at the point where he entered the trail with Jake, which was quite a bit north of where you're suggesting Silvia's captor parked." I looked at Houston. "Sitka would have picked up the scent and followed it to the point where the kidnapper doubled back. I don't think it occurred to any of us that the kidnapper entered the area from somewhere other than the traditionally used parking area."

"It did enter my mind at one point that the kidnapper wouldn't want to take the chance of having his car seen by others hiking in the area, but I wasn't familiar enough with the topography to make a call on where an alternate site might be until we hiked around for a bit."

"Harmony to Jake," I said into my radio.

"Go for Jake."

"Houston has a theory about where Silvia's captor might have taken her." I went through the whole thing step by step, beginning with the alternate parking spot, which would have had Silvia and her captor entering the playing field in a different location.

"That actually makes sense. When we arrived at the place where Sitka picked up the scent, he wanted to go in both directions. If they entered the search grid from a different vantage point and then doubled back, that would explain his behavior. Sitka and I will head back. Unless Yukon picks up on something along the way, plan to meet us at the foot of that little mountain range."

Jake gave instructions to Wyatt and Landon as well and we all set off. Once we reached the foot of the mountains, both dogs were alerting like crazy. It still took another hour to find Silvia bound and gagged on the floor of one of the lower-level mine shafts. She was alive, but just barely. Jake identified a meadow for Dani to land her helicopter, then the entire team worked together to get our victim to the hospital before it was too late.

******

Jake had sent me home once the rescue was complete and the debriefing accomplished. Technically, I had a shift at the bar that night, but he said I looked exhausted and wanted me to get some sleep. Having unscheduled time off was going to wreak havoc on my budget, but I really was tired, and I did have my menagerie to see to. The last thing I wanted to do after a long, steep rescue was take a long walk, but the dogs—other than Yukon, of course—needed to expend some energy, so I layered on some additional clothing against the late-in-the-day chill and went out with all seven dogs in tow.

As I meandered slowly along, enjoying the summer evening, I decided to try once again to call Harley. We'd been playing phone tag a lot as of late, but I wanted to firm up the plans for the fund-raiser and grand opening. I dialed his number with my cell and this time he answered.

"Harmony, I'm glad we finally connected."

I slowed my pace just a bit. "Me too. How are things?"

"Good. I'm pretty exhausted and weary of the constant hustle and bustle of my life in Los Angeles, but we've wrapped up the movie, so once I attend a few more functions my agent scheduled on my behalf, I should be free until the promo tour begins after the first of the year."

"It'll be nice to have you around for a while. Any idea when you might make it back to town? I've been talking to some of the gang at the shelter about holding a grand opening and fund-raiser, but we want to do it when you'll be here."

Harley paused before he answered, maybe to take a minute to check his schedule. "I should be home in a couple of weeks, but you might want to wait until the end of July if you want to be safe. My agent is making noise about me doing a few talk shows before I sequester myself in Alaska for a long-needed break."

I stopped and sat down on a log near a seasonal creek. All seven dogs were happily playing in the water. I'd have to give them a chance to dry off before I let them into the house, but I figured they could just go with me while I saw to the animals in the barn and checked the pen where I hoped to temporarily house the baby moose. If he made it out of the hospital, that is. "Okay," I answered. "I'm sure we can work with a date in late July. We should think about a Saturday if we want to attract people from out of town."

"Did you have a theme in mind?" Harley asked.

"No. We've only just begun to discuss it. Initially, I was just thinking of a small event to announce to the community that we're open for business, but then Serena and I discussed using the event as a fundraiser. It'd be nice to have enough cash in the bank to hire some paid staff."

"If you want to wait until September, I think I can arrange to have Lonesome Moments play."

"Really?" Lonesome Moments was the hottest country band around these days. If they'd agree to play, we'd make enough to staff the shelter through the winter, provided we could find a large enough venue to hold the concert.

"Melissa is coming to Alaska for a month or so after I get home. I'll need to speak to her before we go any further, but I'm willing to bet she'd be happy to help out." Melissa Grainger was the lead singer for Lonesome Moments and, based on what I'd read in the tabloids, Harley's sometime lover. Suddenly, my joy at having such a huge headliner for our little fundraiser was tarnished with jealousy, but I forcefully pushed it aside. Harley and I were just friends. He could have as many gorgeous brunettes stay with him at his isolated estate on the mountain as he wanted.

I tried for a tone of enthusiasm. "That would be great. Really great. Although we'd need to hold the event somewhere other than the shelter."

"Maybe we can hold an open house at the shelter during the day and then have the concert that evening at my place."

"Your place? Are you sure? There will probably be a whole lot of people."

"I'll set up bleachers in one of the pastures and we can have an outdoor concert for the masses, followed by a cocktail reception for a few select guests with deep pockets."

Harley seemed to have it all figured out. Of course, he went to fund-raisers all the time, while I'd been to exactly zero.

"So, how are things otherwise?" he asked after we finished discussing the specifics of the suddenly huge event that seemed to have popped up from nowhere. I was feeling a bit overwhelmed.

"I guess you haven't heard about Pastor Brown," I said.

"Heard?" Harley's voice demonstrated curiosity. "Did something happen to him?"

I filled him in on the pastor's death and the kidnapping of one of Rescue's long-term residents, as well as the theory that we'd most likely find a link between them.

"Wow," Harley said. "I can't believe something like that could happen in Rescue. Who would do such a thing?"

"I have no idea. Pastor Brown has been a community leader ever since I can remember. I didn't belong to his church, so I didn't know him well, but everyone I've spoken to is shocked beyond belief."

"I'm sorry, Harm. I'm sure this must be difficult for you. Is there anything I can do?"

I wanted to suggest he rush home and hold my hand, but I didn't. "No. I'm fine."

"Listen, I'm sorry to cut this short, but the reporter is here for the interview my agent set up."

"You're being interviewed at this time of night?"

"Los Angeles is a twenty-four-hour town. I was busy for most of the day, so she graciously agreed to come by my place this evening. I'll try to call you later. And Harmony…"

"Yeah?"

"I'm sorry again about Pastor Brown. If you need me, whether it's to brainstorm or just to talk, call me. Anytime. I'll try to keep an eye out for your number."

I couldn't help but smile. "Thanks, Harley. Enjoy the rest of your evening and let me know right away if you firm things up with Melissa Grainger. We'll want to start promoting the event right away."

I hung up, then called the dogs to my side and headed back home. As I'd planned, I had them come into the barn with me so they had time to at least partially dry off before I let them into the house. Once the barn was cleaned and the barn animals fed, I took the five house dogs back to the cabin and fed them as well. I popped a frozen dinner into the microwave while I cleaned cat boxes, then settled in with my frozen dinner and a glass of wine. By the time I'd eaten, fatigue was beginning to set in, so I cleaned up the kitchen, then went to bed.

I slowly sat up on what must have been a mattress tossed on the ground. I couldn't see anything in the windowless room, but I could feel something on the bed next to me. My hands, which had been bound, were freed, allowing me to pick up the object, which turned out to be a flashlight. I turned it on and looked around in horror. I was somewhere underground. The air was stale, the walls made of dirt and rock, so I assumed I was in a cave of some sort. I was no longer as dizzy as I had been when I'd first arrived, but my mouth was dry and the knot in my stomach felt as real as it ever had. Once my eyes adjusted to the dim light, I noticed a tray off to the side of the mattress. It held a glass of water and a loaf of bread. I had enough presence of mind to wonder if they'd been poisoned, but my throat was so dry that not taking a drink wasn't an option. I sipped the water slowly and ate part of the bread as I tried to figure out my next move. I'd started to get up when I heard a loud noise. I turned toward it, and everything went black.

I screamed as I struggled to consciousness. As I had been the last time I'd had the dream, I was bathed in sweat, my bedclothes twisted and tangled around my body. I threw my blankets to the floor, then sat up and placed my feet on the floor. My heart was racing so I waited to stand.

"It's okay," I said to the dogs, who were once again running around and barking. "It was just a dream. A very bad dream."

Honey crawled into my lap. I buried my face in her thick fur and let the tears come. The dream had been similar to the one I'd had the previous night, but this time instead of observing a woman who had been trapped in a cave from a distance, it felt like I was the one going through the experience. I forced my mind to look back as I tried to remember the two dreams. Both were in cold, dark locations. Both featured a captive who had been brought there while unconscious, and in both dreams, the victim's wrists had been bound at one point. Could they be visions, not dreams at all? The thought had entered my mind as we looked for Silvia. Of course, a vision had to be of someone who'd been taken before last night and was still being held this evening.

I glanced at the clock. It was much too late to call anyone. I hadn't heard about any missing persons, so I doubted I was dealing with visions. Still, it wouldn't hurt to talk to Jake, see what he thought about them.

Once my heart stopped racing, I slowly stood and went into the bathroom. I washed my face, then changed my pj's and bedding. I grabbed a glass of water and took it into the living room. I sat down on my sofa and let the dogs surround me. After I reassured everyone that I was fine, I went to look for Denali, who was staring out the same window he'd been staring out the previous night.

"What do you see?" I asked as fingers of fear tickled their way up my spine.

Denali didn't move, and everything about his stance and demeanor led me to believe he was locked onto something I couldn't see. The idea that there could be someone out there waiting and watching caused my stomach to twist and rumble. Sleep, I realized, would no longer be an option, so I grabbed a quilt, then curled up on the sofa with my guardians to wait until the summer sun showed its face over the horizon.

Chapter 5

Wednesday, June 20

Surprisingly, I actually managed to catch some sleep after I'd settled in front of the television to wait for daybreak. By the time I awoke it was after eight o'clock. As I did every morning, I started my day by walking the dogs. It was a beautiful day, the sun warm and welcoming and the meadow brilliant with wildflowers. As he had the previous day, Denali stayed close to my side rather than running ahead, but Yukon and Shia were just as happy leading the pack. Honey and Lucky didn't seem to mind that Denali had joined them at the back and made room for him next to my left thigh.

"You know I'll be perfectly fine if you want to run on ahead," I said to Denali, who seemed more focused on the woods around us than he was on me or the other dogs walking with us. "You don't want Yukon to get the idea he's the alpha dog now. He's still a pup, and so is Shia, but it won't be long before he'll be looking to establish his own place in our little pack."

Denali glanced at me as if to acknowledge that he'd heard what I was trying to communicate, then went back to scanning the forest. I tried to relax and let the warmth of the sun chase away the tightness in my neck and shoulders. I had a lot to get done today and I needed to be at my best, despite the feeling of terror that lingered after the very realistic dreams I'd had the previous two nights.

As I strolled along and mentally outlined my day, I realized I should call Chloe. She wasn't going to be happy if she had to find out about Silvia's kidnapping from Raelene. I also needed to check in with Kelly about the baby moose and the dog who'd had surgery. I might need to bring the dog to my place while he recovered. I had a spare room. I supposed I could make up a bed for him in there.

I was about to call Yukon and Shia back when Denali started to growl from deep in his chest. I paused to look around. I didn't see or hear anything. Again, I opened my mouth to call Yukon and Shia back when I heard barking from up ahead. Denali hadn't moved. He continued to growl but didn't take off as he had the first time. I supposed we were in about the same spot we'd been when he'd taken off before but had no idea what was upsetting the dogs so. Lucky and Honey were literally sitting on my feet when Juno and Kodi came running back to me. I let out a loud whistle to call Yukon and Shia back, which they responded to. I took a final look around, then started back to the house.

I wondered if I should come back with only Denali to take a better look around. I hadn't seen any sign of a trespasser, but then again, I hadn't looked all that hard either. During the winter, when the snow lay heavy on the ground, it was easy to spot the presence of anyone who might venture too close to my cabin by searching for footprints. At this time of the year, however, I'd need to depend on subtler clues like broken twigs and mashed-down grass.

At the cabin, I fed the dogs, then saw to my phone calls. Kelly reported that the baby moose was doing much better and had real hope for him now that he seemed to have taken to the artificial milk she'd been feeding him around the clock. She asked once again if I'd be able to take him once he was medically stable, and I assured her I could and would. I had no idea how I'd adjust my schedule to include around-the-clock feedings, but I'd done it in the past with other young and ill rescues and I'd find a way to do it again. As for the dog who'd had surgery, Justine was going to take him home with her until he recovered. Now that, I mused, was service above and beyond the call of duty.

After I hung up with Kelly, I thought about calling Chloe but decided I'd shower and dress for the day, then drop in on her café for breakfast and share the details about Silvia's kidnapping in person.

******

Chloe's Café was a locals' hangout, so I should have anticipated it would be crowded at this time of the day. I waved to Chloe, who was taking the order from a large group, then indicated I'd take a seat at the counter. Perhaps this hadn't been the best idea after all. It would be hard to fill Chloe in on the details of the kidnapping with so many people within hearing range. Maybe I could pull her aside if there was a lull in the action at some point. Even if she didn't have time to really discuss what had happened, I'd get points for sharing what I knew before she heard it from anyone else.

"Morning, Susan," I said as I slid onto the stool next to one of the women who sometimes worked the counter at the local minimart.

"Morning, Harmony. After all your excitement yesterday, I didn't expect you to be up and about so early this morning."

"All my excitement?" I asked, hoping she was referring to something other than the search for and eventual recovery of Silvia White.

"You don't need to pretend with me. I know you aren't supposed to discuss the things you do as a search-and-rescue team member, but it's all over town that Silvia White was kidnapped and left for dead in a mine shaft."

I glanced at Chloe, who was talking to Ryan McGowan from the bank. She didn't look mad, but with her, you couldn't always tell.

"I'm curious where you picked up this piece of information," I said to Susan.

"Jackie Portman told everyone at spin class this morning. I'm not sure where she heard it, but the word must have leaked early because class starts at seven and several of the women had already heard about Silvia before Jackie said anything." Susan took a sip of her coffee. "You know how it is when you live in a small town. You can't sneeze without everyone asking if you have a cold."

"I guess you aren't wrong about that." I motioned for the waitress working the counter to bring me a cup of coffee when she had a chance.

"The word around town is that Silvia's kidnapping and Pastor Brown's murder were carried out by the same person," Susan added.

"I suppose that's a possibility," I commented. "Do you have any idea why anyone would want to harm both Silvia and Pastor Brown?"

Susan cocked her head to the side as if to consider my question. "Not really. They both lived in Rescue for a really long time. Silvia attends the pastor's church, so they knew each other. In fact, it seems to me Silvia volunteers at the church from time to time. Both seem like nice folks who wouldn't hurt a flea. Any way you look at it, the whole thing seems pretty senseless."

"I agree." I took a sip of my coffee. "It doesn't make a bit of sense." I took another sip and narrowed my gaze. "Can you think of anyone who might have some insight into what was going on in either of their lives?"

"Have you heard whether Silvia has regained consciousness?" Susan asked.

"Not as of this morning. Her injuries turned out to be extensive, so she's been transferred to the hospital in Anchorage, where she can get the specialized care she needs."

Susan turned slightly to look me in the eye. "If I were the one looking in to things, I'd speak to Pastor Brown's secretary for sure. Secretaries usually are in the know even more than wives about what's going on in their bosses' lives. Of course, Pastor Brown was a widower, so there isn't a wife to talk to."

"That's a good suggestion. I seem to remember Ilse Baldwin is the church secretary."

"Yes, Ilse took over after Veronica left. She technically works for the church, so she might even be in her office today despite the pastor's death. I'm sure there are arrangements to be made and she'd likely be the one to make them."

"I'll stop by to speak to her after I leave here. How about Silvia?"

"How about Silvia what?" Chloe said as she slipped up to the counter and gave me a hug. At least she didn't seem mad.

"We were just discussing who might be able to provide some insight into the lives of Rescue's two most recent crime victims," Susan said.

"I came to tell you," I quickly added. "I'm sorry I didn't get here before you heard."

Chloe waved her hand. "Don't worry about it. I was insane yesterday. I mean, really, what was I thinking to yell at you like that? If I were you, I'd dump me as your best friend. But please don't," she added quickly.

"I'd never dump you. I need you to help keep me grounded."

"Charmayne Pewter," Susan said suddenly.

I turned away from Chloe and looked at Susan. "Charmayne?"

"Charmayne and Silvia are great friends. I bet if there's something going on in Silvia's life, Charmayne would know."

"I don't suppose you have her phone number?" I asked Susan.

"Better. She's working at the visitor center for the summer. I'm pretty sure you'll be able to find her there if you stop by before five."

"This whole thing is just so upsetting," Chloe said. "I know we made some comments yesterday about not being alone, but now that two members of our community have been the victim of senseless violence, I'm not so sure we were wise to discount the idea so quickly. Do you think there's some wacko out there kidnapping people at random?"

I didn't know, but I certainly hoped not.

When I left the café, I headed toward the church. I didn't know if anyone would be on the premises today, but it wasn't much out of my way, so it couldn't hurt to check. Ilse Baldwin was a logical, organized, focused woman. She ran the church finances with a tight fist, as well as the schedules and weekly meetings. On Sunday mornings Pastor Brown was in charge as he ministered to his congregation, but the rest of the week it was Ilse who ran things. When I arrived at the church office, I found her on the phone. She motioned for me to take a seat while she finished her call. I'd half-expected her to have taken some time off given the circumstances, but from what I could hear from her side of the call, it sounded as if she was lining up a guest pastor for the following Sunday.

"Thank you for waiting," Ilse said as soon as she hung up. "How can I help you?"

"I guess you know that I, as a member of the search-and-rescue team, was the one who found Pastor Brown's body."

Ilse nodded. "Yes, I'm aware of that."

"I'm here now to ask you about him in the weeks preceding his death. Was he distracted, or did he seem overly stressed?"

She pursed her lips. "Aren't these the sort of questions the police should be asking?"

"They are," I admitted. "And they very well may be. It's just that after I found Silvia half dead in the mine yesterday, I had the feeling there was someone else I was supposed to help. The problem is, I can't make a clear connection. I hoped if I can figure out why Pastor Brown and Silvia were targeted, I might be able to figure out who this third person might be."

Ilse crossed her arms across her chest as she looked me up and down. I could understand her hesitation. Asking questions relating to Pastor Brown's death wasn't my job, and while Ilse and I were acquaintances, it wasn't as if we were good friends who might share confidences.

"I'm not sure I should be talking to you about this," she said at last, "but I've heard about your unique talent, and I guess there really could be someone in need of your help. I wish I had a logical explanation about why Pastor Brown was killed, but I don't. Although…"

"Although?"

"The pastor came back to the office after his dinner in town on Sunday. I'd stopped in to pick up a list of florists I was working on getting bids from and noticed he was at his desk. I asked him why he was working on what should have been his evening off, and he said he wanted to make some notes for his sermon next week."

"Was that unusual?" I asked.

"Sure. Why would he need to come to his office to make notes? I'm certain he had notepads, pens, and a computer in his office at home."

"Maybe he needed reference material he didn't have at home," I suggested.

"Perhaps. But I noticed something else. Something I found to be both unusual and alarming."

"And what was that?"

"He had a glass on his desk. I'm certain it was filled with brandy. Now, it wasn't that the man was a teetotaler. He was known to have a brandy in the evening every now and then. But he never drank here in the church offices. Or at least not as far as I knew. And it wasn't only the brandy I found odd; it was his demeanor. His sermon that morning had been well received, so you'd think he would have been in a good mood, but he was quiet and introspective. He barely said two words to me, and those two words were delivered in a monotone."

"So you think he had something heavy on his mind?"

"That would be my guess, although he didn't say what might have been bothering him and it's too late to ask him now."

"Did you notice anything else on his desk? A file or a photograph?"

Ilse shook her head. "No. He was just sitting in his chair, staring into space. I didn't push for an explanation, but now I wish I had."

"Pastor Brown had dinner with Jolene Pinewood and her family on Sunday. He told her that he'd arranged to meet someone he knew from the past. Did he say anything to you that might indicate who it was he was meeting?"

"He didn't say a word about it. And I'm quite certain there was no Sunday evening meeting on the official schedule. I would have remembered that."

"What time would you say it was you were here on Sunday?"

"I guess around five."

I knew Pastor Brown had been at the Pinewood house until four. Had he come to his office after meeting whoever it was he'd been seeing or before?

Ilse and I spoke for a few more minutes and then I headed back to the shelter. Now that we were officially open for business, it was important for volunteers to show up and do what they'd committed to do. As quasi head of the shelter and the volunteers, I wanted to be sure I set a good example.

By the time I arrived, the other volunteers were there, the cages had been cleaned, and the animals in our care had been fed and exercised.

"Oh good, you're here," one of them said. "We've been discussing the possibility of running an adoption clinic in Fairbanks in a few weeks. The number of animals in need compared to the number of prospective people looking for a pet is going to make placing our wards difficult unless we widen our population pool."

"I think holding a clinic in the city is a good idea. Serena and I spoke yesterday about having a grand opening and fund-raiser after Harley gets back in town. We might want to do that first because the event could generate local adoptions." I didn't want to spill the beans about Melissa yet. "Harley and I are looking at a date in September. When I have more information, I'll let you know."

Everyone agreed holding the local event first was a good plan. We were discussing possible themes for it when a young woman came in with six kittens. I let the others handle the admittance while I went to check on the animals we already had. I wasn't needed at the shelter, so I decided to head over to the visitor center to try to catch Charmayne Pewter. She'd only lived in Rescue for about two years, but she gave extensively of her time and talent, and most considered Rescue to have benefited from her move to town. She'd been a history teacher before she retired and had boned up on local history, so she provided a new perspective to everyone who stopped by for coupons and recommendations.

"Morning, Charmayne."

"Harmony, I'm so glad you're here. I planned to call you later. I'm just so devastated about what happened to poor Silvia. Who would do such a thing?"

"I don't know," I responded. "I was sort of hoping you would."

Charmayne put a hand to her chest. "How would I know anything about Silvia's kidnapping?"

"I just thought maybe Silvia had said or done something in the days leading up to it that might shed some light on what sort of trouble she was in."

Charmayne lifted a brow. "So you think Silvia was kidnapped and left to die because of something she did?"

That wasn't exactly what I meant, but I could see how it sounded that way. "I mean the odds are someone in her life, someone she knew, did this. I'm just trying to figure out the who and the why. I'm just trying to help," I emphasized.

Charmayne sat down on a stool behind the counter. "I spoke to Sil's sister this morning. She said she's still unconscious." A tear trailed down her slightly wrinkled cheek. "She said she might not ever wake up. I don't understand how this could have happened."

I leaned my arms on the counter and gave her a sympathetic look. "I understand your grief. I don't know Silvia well, but she's lived in Rescue since before I was born, and she's served her community well. Whoever is responsible needs to be brought to justice. I can't believe there isn't someone who saw or heard something that will point us in a direction. If Silvia said anything at all to you, even something that seems very minor, about something she planned to do or was on her mind, it could help us find the answer."

"Okay." Charmayne seemed to have come to a decision. She got up, crossed to the door, and turned the Open sign to Closed. She led me into a back room that served as a staff lounge. She pointed to a chair at a small table, then poured us each a cup of coffee from the pot. "I did speak to Silvia at yoga yesterday. She came with Lisa Long, who had to leave early because her husband called to say their baby had a fever and he couldn't get her to stop crying. After Lisa left, I offered Silvia a ride home, but she said she'd arranged to have breakfast with an old acquaintance and would ask him to drive her home afterward. We left together, and I went to the parking lot to pick up my car. Just as I was pulling out, I saw a dark blue car pull up to the curb. Silvia got in and the car sped away."

"Did you catch the license plate number?"

"No. I wasn't paying that much attention and didn't notice, but I think it was a rental."

"Did you see the driver?"

"Not really. I seem to remember dark hair, but that's about it."

"When Silvia told you that she was having breakfast with this friend, how did she seem? Excited? Nervous?"

Charmayne screwed up her face as she appeared to be considering my question. "Not exactly excited or nervous really. She did seem cautious. Perhaps even a bit apprehensive. She was careful to say she was having breakfast with an old *acquaintance*. Her reluctance to use the word friend seemed deliberate. I thought to myself it might be one of her old patients who was in town and wanted to catch up. That happens from time to time, you know. Men and women who are helped by doctors have been known to form an unnatural attachment. Silvia was much too polite to turn down invitations when offered, but I do know that at times she found them to be a burden."

"So, it's possible the person who picked Silvia up was a former patient?"

"Sure. It's possible, but I don't know that for certain. We only spoke for as long as it took for Silvia to very politely tell me that she didn't need a ride home."

I stood up and prepared to go.

"Avis," Charmayne said.

"Avis?"

"The car had a license plate holder from Avis. I have no idea which Avis office, but I suppose Avis is a lead."

I nodded. "It is. Thank you. And if you think of anything else, please call me."

Avis wasn't a lot to go on, but it was something. I figured Officer Houston might be able to turn that small tip into a real clue. I could simply have called the police station to relay my bit of information, but after working with Officer Houston the day before, I was somewhat curious about one of Rescue's newest residents. It wouldn't take long to stop by to see if he was in. If he wasn't, I could always leave the information with whoever was on duty.

"Ms. Carson, how can I help you?" Officer Houston asked after I was shown to his office by the woman who was working the reception counter.

I sat down opposite him at his desk. "I happened onto a small piece of information I thought you might find useful. According to Silvia's friend, Charmayne Pewter, the car the man who picked Silvia up from yoga was driving had an Avis license plate holder. We don't have a car rental place in town, but there's one at the airport in Fairbanks."

Houston steepled his fingers across the front of his chest, a little smile on his face. "That's very helpful. We have the make, model, and color. It shouldn't be too hard to get a list of men who rented a dark blue Ford Focus from Avis. Good work."

I couldn't help but grin.

"I'm glad you stopped by. I was very impressed with your ability to find that woman yesterday. I have to say, when Jake first told me about your gift, I was skeptical, but after seeing you in action, I'm willing to say I've never seen anything like it."

"Sometimes a gift and sometimes a curse, but thank you. It does feel good when we get to the victim in time."

"Can you do that any time you want? Find a missing person with little more than a name?"

I shook my head. "No. Not always. I can usually see people who are relatively nearby and in need of rescue. The more information I have, the more likely I can get a connection. I know Silvia, so that made it easier. To now, I've only connected with people in need of rescue. It's not like I can walk down the street and read everyone's mind. It's pretty selective."

"Well, I'm glad to know that if I go up backcountry skiing and get lost, you'll come fetch me."

I laughed. "Trust me, you don't want to get lost in the backcountry. It's best to take a guide who knows the terrain. I can only connect with people who are alive, and a lot of folks who go without a guide don't stay alive long enough for me to find them."

"Good to know, and thanks for the tip."

"If you're serious about going, talk to Dani Mathews. She teams up with local guides and provides tours to people wanting a real backwoods experience." I stood up. "I should go. Thank you for your time."

"Before you go, as long as you're giving me newcomer advice, can you recommend a good Italian restaurant?"

"There aren't a lot of options for dinner in Rescue. Sarge, the cook at Neverland, can do justice to any dish he prepares. I suppose if you want Italian, he'd be able to prepare something for you. I work the dinner shift tonight. If you want to come by, I'll introduce you. If Sarge likes you, he'll make you anything you want."

"Thanks. I just might do that."

I didn't know why the thought made me so happy. It shouldn't have. Hank Houston was an outsider who apparently had a wild hair to rough it here in Alaska for reasons known only to him. There was no way he was dating material, any more than Harley was. One was a superstar who would never settle full-time in Rescue, the other was a townie who'd probably run back to Boston with his tail between his legs once the long nights of winter hit. No, I decided, what I needed, if I decided I even needed a man, was someone local who knew how to survive the snow, the cold, the dark, and the isolation, and had put down roots here because of, not despite, the unique lifestyle that could only be found in the forty-ninth state.

Chapter 6

Although Neverland was intended to be a bar first and a restaurant second, it was the food that brought the locals in during the off season, which included pretty much every month of the year other than July and August. My shift normally ran from four to midnight, although during the winter, the bar tended to empty out early, so Jake, in turn, closed early.

"I need two prime rib specials, two cheeseburgers, and a baked halibut with mashed potatoes," I said to Sarge, who was manning the kitchen as he did every night the bar was open.

"I've got your salmon burger and halibut sandwich ready. Did they want potato salad or coleslaw?"

"Both want slaw and beans. It's busy tonight. Wyatt has the bar covered and you seem to be holding your own in the kitchen, but I could use some help on the floor. Do you know if Jake has anyone else coming in?" I asked.

"Jake went to Fairbanks with Jordan, but he said he'd be back before things got too crazy." Sarge frowned as he set two plates piled high with food on the counter. "I'm kind of surprised he isn't here by now. I hope there wasn't an accident on the road."

"I'll call him when I get a minute. The couple who's splitting the chef salad would also like garlic bread. Do you have any made tonight?"

"I just need to heat it up. We're running low on ribs, so don't push them. We have plenty of pot roast, so mention that instead in your spiel."

I smiled at the grizzly man behind the kitchen window. Sarge was ex-military, tattooed and worn, with a balding head and leathery skin from long days under the desert sun, yet beneath his rough exterior was the sweetest man you were ever likely to meet. "I'll deliver these, then come back for the salads for table ten. The four top in the corner is ready for dessert. Is there any chocolate cake left?"

"Two slices," Sarge responded. "I have a nice cherry cobbler."

"Okay, I'll see if they want something." I grabbed the plates Sarge had ready and headed out to deliver them.

The next three hours were crazy busy, but then, just as quickly as the place filled up, it emptied out. I never had gotten around to calling Jake, so I did so now. My call went to voicemail, so I went to the bar for a much-needed diet cola.

"Weird that Jake didn't show," Wyatt commented as he slid my glass across the bar.

"Yeah." I frowned. "It's not like him not to call. I hope everything's okay. It's been clear all day, so the weather shouldn't have been a problem."

"I'm sure everything is fine. Seems like things are steaming up a bit between him and Jordan. My guess would be that they decided to get a room in Fairbanks for the night."

I tilted my head. "I kind of doubt that. And if they did decide to stay, why wouldn't Jake call?"

"You did hear me say extra steamy?" Wyatt chuckled.

I rolled my eyes. I was happy Jake and Jordan seemed to be taking their relationship to the next level. Val had been gone a long time, and I wanted Jake to be happy. But if Wyatt was right and Jake had decided to take an unscheduled night off on the same night pretty much everyone in town came in for dinner, I wasn't going to be happy. Though if he had an excuse like having been in an accident, that wouldn't make me happy either.

There were just two tables who were still eating when Officer Houston wandered in. "I was just about to give up on you," I teased as I showed him to one of our nicest tables, next to a window overlooking the lake.

"I intended to come in earlier, but there was an accident on the highway."

"Jake?" I gasped.

"Jake was there. So was Jordan. In fact, it was Jordan's timely response that saved the woman's life. But don't worry; neither of them was involved in the accident. They just happened to come upon it shortly after it occurred."

I let out a long breath. "I'm glad they weren't involved. Jake was supposed to come in to help this evening, and when he didn't show, I started to worry. I'm glad he's okay."

"Jordan went with the female victim to the hospital and Jake followed with the truck they'd been traveling in. I'm sure he'll check in with you the minute he has the opportunity."

"I'm sure he will. So, what can I get you to drink?"

"Coffee would be great."

"Okay, I'll get that while you look at the menu. I'll check with Sarge to see what he has left in terms of tonight's specials."

I shared with Wyatt what Officer Houston had told me about Jake and Jordan and asked him to deliver a pot of coffee to his table, then went to the kitchen to talk to Sarge. "We have a new customer tonight: Officer Houston. He asked about Italian food earlier in the day, although I'm not sure that's still what he has in mind. What do you have left of the specials?"

"Ribs."

I crossed my arms over my chest. "I thought we were out of ribs."

"I said we were low so not to push them. You didn't push them, so now we have ribs. I can make him a scampi with saffron, asparagus, and angel hair if he's still craving something with an Italian flair. If he wants to give me some notice, I'll bake a lasagna later in the week."

"Okay. I'll let him know. By the way, he also told me that Jake's late because he and Jordan stopped to help a woman who'd been injured in an accident. I doubt he'll be in tonight, but the rush seems to be over, so I should be fine."

After I shared the specials with Officer Houston, as well as Sarge's offer to make the scampi, he chose the latter. By the time I'd placed Houston's order, the two tables who had been finishing up were ready for checks. I cashed them out, then wandered over to Houston's table with a basket of bread and a fresh green salad with Sarge's homemade dressing.

"Sarge said to tell you that if you give him a bit of notice, he can bake a lasagna for you later in the week."

"I love lasagna. Tell him to let me know what day he wants to make it and I'll be here. In fact, I'll probably start coming in on a regular basis, now that I know you serve real food, not just bar food."

"I'm sure the two of you will get along just fine."

"Join me," Houston offered as he started in on his salad.

"Join you?"

"The place has cleared out. At least for now. And I'd welcome someone to chat with while I eat. You can tell me about the S-and-R team. Besides, eating alone is the worst thing about being new to town and not knowing anyone."

I glanced at Wyatt. He'd turned the TV on to ESPN. "Okay. But just until someone comes in. Let me grab a soda."

After I poured myself another diet cola, I sat down across from Houston. If he wanted someone to talk to, I'd take advantage of the opportunity to get some information out of him as well. "So, Officer Houston, other than that you aren't a fan of eating alone, how are you liking our little town?"

"Hank."

I lifted a brow.

"When I'm not acting in an official capacity, I prefer it if people call me Hank."

"I think I'll stick to Houston for the time being."

He shrugged. "Whatever floats your boat. And I'm enjoying my time here more than I thought I would."

I leaned back and crossed my arms over my stomach. "You took a job in Rescue, but you didn't think you'd enjoy living here?"

Houston chuckled again. "I guess that is the way it sounded. It isn't that I didn't expect to like it here exactly. I needed a change and this job came up, so I applied. I guess I didn't stop to think about how I'd like living way out here in the middle of nowhere. When I first arrived and had a look around, I was certain I wouldn't last a month, but it's been a month and I've settled in and I can actually see myself living here."

"I see." I figured a man doesn't move from Boston to a tiny town in northern Alaska without a better reason than needing a change. I knew there was a story there, but I'd let it go for now. "Rescue's a pretty big change from Boston."

"I'd say that's an understatement. But I've found the people to be warm and welcoming, and up until the past couple of days, the toughest case I've had to deal with was breaking up a drunken brawl between the Baxter twins."

Now it was my turn to laugh. "Tank and Tanner Baxter certainly are an interesting pair. They fight more than any two people I've ever known, but when push comes to shove, they have each other's back."

"I could see that when I tossed them in my one and only jail cell until they sobered up. One minute they wanted to kill each other, the next they were teaming up to kill me instead. If I hadn't had my gun on me, I think I might have been in real trouble."

"They might have punched you a few times, but they wouldn't have actually killed you. In the future, if you need a way to break them up without having to arrest them, call their mama. They do what she says whether they're drunk or not."

"And does this mama have a name?"

"Trudy. Trudy Baxter. She owns the only tow truck in town."

"Are you talking about that tiny little thing who changed my carburetor when I first came to town?"

"That'd be her. She can't weigh more than ninety pounds soaking wet, but don't let her size fool you. She's as tough as they come. Strong too."

"How did such a tiny woman have two such huge sons?" Houston wondered.

"Her ex was a big man. I guess the boys take after him in terms of size, but there's no doubt they're Trudy's boys if you're taking in to account orneriness and determination."

"Are you trying to say that sweet little Trudy has a dark side?"

"And how. She can be sweet as pie, but if you end up on her wrong side, she'll tear you a new one before you even know what's happened. She won't tolerate any nonsense, but as long as she's on your side, she can be a real asset."

Houston pushed his empty salad plate to the side. "Good to know. I guess I should have had dinner with you sooner. It's helpful to get the lay of the land, so to speak."

"I've lived here all my life. Anything you want to know, just ask."

"You married?" Houston asked.

I was surprised by the question but recovered quickly enough not to let it show. "I am most definitely not married."

Houston raised a brow. "Seems there's more going on in that statement than one could decipher from words alone."

"You'll just need to get to know me better and decide for yourself. How about you? I haven't seen a wife in tow since you've arrived in town, so I'm going to assume you aren't currently married. Ever been?"

"Once, but I quickly learned that being a cop who's often forced into dangerous situations and having a wife who tends to stress out about them aren't a good mix. She wanted me to give up the job, but I decided it would be easier to give up the wife."

"Any kids?"

"No. It was just the two of us."

"Then it seems you made the right choice. There are worse things than being alone. Not that I really know what that's like, given the menagerie I live with. Do you have any pets?"

Houston shook his head. "No. It's just me."

"Seems like the chief of police should have a dog." I paused to give it some thought. "There's a shepherd at the shelter with a lot of possibilities. He's young, energetic, and smart. If you're interested, I'd be willing to throw in some specialized training as part of the deal."

"Do you normally pawn off strays on people you've just met?"

"Absolutely. If I come across someone who's a good fit for one of my strays, I can be pushy as all get out. And honestly, I think you and Kojak will get on fine."

Houston hesitated, but he didn't say no right away, so I figured he might be intrigued by the idea.

"Come by the shelter tomorrow morning and I'll introduce you," I added. "If you and Kojak get along as well as I think you will, we can discuss the specifics."

"Okay."

Wow. That was easier than I thought.

"On one condition."

"Which is?"

"If we do like each other and I do decide to adopt him, you have to be the one to see to his training. I've never had a dog before and, quite frankly, I wouldn't know what to do with an intelligent, energetic shepherd."

I held out my hand. "It's a deal. Kojak is smart. Once you establish yourself as the alpha, the rest will come easily." I glanced toward the kitchen. "It looks like your meal is up. Do you need anything else to drink?"

Houston glanced at the bar. "I suppose I'm off duty, and I am having Italian. Perhaps a glass of cabernet?"

"One glass of house cab coming right up."

After I delivered the wine to Houston's table, several parties came in for drinks and appetizers. By the time I got them taken care of, Houston had finished his meal. He seemed delighted with it, so I introduced him to Sarge, who doesn't understand the art of a brief conversation, so I left them together while I finished my shift. I'd wanted to have the chance to talk to Jake about my dream, so I hoped he'd be in before I left at midnight. Houston must have snuck out when I was busy because I never actually saw him leave, but I did know he'd been chatting with Sarge for at least an hour by the time he finally made his excuses and took off.

"Looks like you found yourself a nice young man," Sarge said as I delivered the last of the dishes to the kitchen.

"I didn't find him because he wasn't lost, he is in no way mine, and I don't think he's all that young."

Sarge chuckled. "All the same, based on what I've learned, I like him, and you know I don't usually warm up to strangers right away."

I began to fill the sink with soap and water. "I'm well aware of your tendency to be discriminating, and I like him too. I have a feeling there's more going on than meets the eye when it comes to his reason for being in Rescue, but I'll give him the benefit of the doubt for now. Have you heard from Jake?"

"He's on his way in. He was going to drop Jordan at her place and then come to the bar to help with the cleanup."

"Did he say how things went with the woman Jordan helped at the scene of the accident?"

"He said she's going to be all right. I can do those dishes if you want to head home. You look exhausted."

I dipped my hands into the hot, sudsy water. There was something almost calming about scrubbing pans after a long, stressful day. "Thanks, but I really want to talk to Jake. Wyatt is closing out the cash register, but I think he plans to split when he's done. I never did have dinner. What do you have left that's cooked and ready to eat?"

"I have ribs in the warmer and baked beans in the pan."

"Perfect. Make me up a plate. I'll eat it after I finish these pans."

Jake had arrived by the time I'd finished the dishes and settled in at the bar to eat my dinner. He hadn't had a chance to eat either, so he grabbed a plate of food and joined me. We invited Sarge to join us, but he said he was exhausted and went up to his room above the bar.

"Sarge said the woman you stopped to help is going to be okay. I'm glad to hear it," I said as I sucked BBQ sauce from my fingers.

"Thanks to Jordan. She's really amazing. If she hadn't been there, that woman would have died. It was touch-and-go there for a while."

I tried licking the BBQ sauce from my chin, but my tongue wouldn't reach, so I just kept eating. "Jordan is amazing. In fact, she's one of my very favorite people. I'm glad the two of you are allowing your relationship to evolve. You're good together."

Jake paused to look at me. "I know you've said you're fine with me and Jordan, but are you really?"

I shrugged. "Of course. She's great. Why wouldn't I be anything other than happy for both of you?"

"I was married to your sister. I just thought it might be weird for you to see me getting serious with someone else."

I set down my rib and used my napkin to wipe my face. "Val loved you, and I know you loved her, but she's dead. She'd want you to be happy. I want you to be happy."

Jake nodded. "Okay. As long as you're sure. Jordan and I have been friends for a long time, and I really do think there could be something more between us, but it's important to me that you and I are okay."

"We're fine. I promise." I started on my baked beans while Jake told me about the climbing gear he and Jordan had been looking at for the S-and-R team. A lot of our rescues during the summer were of climbers who didn't have the experience they should have before tackling our mountains. Wyatt was the best climber on the team, followed by Jake and Dani. Austin was getting pretty good as well, and while Landon was the brains of the operation, he had recently taken up climbing and, like me, could hold his own. The only S-and-R team member who refused to even try was Jordan, but her job was to patch up those we rescued, so it all worked out in the end.

I still intended to talk to Jake about my dreams, but I wanted to wait until he'd had a chance to eat before bringing up such a disturbing subject. He'd stopped talking to finish up his last couple of bites, so I jumped in. "I've had nightmares the last two nights in a row."

Jake paused. "Nightmares? About Val?"

"No, not about Val. I'm not sure who they're about, to be honest. There's a woman who seems to be trapped in a dark space. Completely dark. It's cold and damp, so I'm thinking she might be being held in a mine or cave, or maybe even an underground cellar. The woman is terrified. The air is stale and the scents around her are overwhelming."

"You sound like you're describing a vision, not a dream."

"It feels like a vision, although I'm asleep. The dreams are so real, I wake up screaming, as if I'm the one trapped in this dark, airless space."

Jake pushed his plate to the side. "You said the dreams started two nights ago?"

I nodded. "On Monday. At first, I figured the dream could have been brought on by Pastor Brown's death. Looking back now, that doesn't really make sense. The pastor was murdered, but there was nothing to indicate he'd been held in a place like the dream at any point. Then, last night, I had the dream again, only this time instead of observing the woman in the dark room, I felt like I *was* her."

"We did find Silvia in a cave, and it was dark and cold," Jake said gently.

"I know. By then, the location of the dream made more sense. But there was more. In addition to experiencing the dream as if I were the woman in it, I had a flashlight, which wasn't there the first night, as well as a loaf of bread and a glass of water. I suppose I could have created them subconsciously, looking for a solution to my dilemma. But it seemed so real. So very, very, real."

"It's possible that finding Silvia hidden away in a cave could have amplified the dream you'd had the night before. Plus, if you didn't sleep well on Monday you must have been exhausted by Tuesday, which could have heightened your emotional connection to everything in it."

"Maybe. But the dreams felt more like the visions I experience in real time. Of course, I've never had visions while asleep before."

"If your dreams are visions, there may be a third victim," Jake stated.

"I think it's something worth exploring. The first dream was on Monday night, so if it was a vision, it couldn't have been of Silvia because she hadn't been kidnapped yet. I think at a minimum, we should check missing persons reports. If it *is* a vision, the woman's being held close by. My visions are usually only of those in close proximity."

"I'll talk to Officer Houston tomorrow, have him run a missing persons report. If you have the dream again, write down everything you can remember the minute you wake up."

That was a good suggestion. As real as the dreams seemed while I was asleep, by the next morning they'd faded into distant memory.

It was after one when I got home. I let the dogs out for a quick run while I fed the animals in the barn. The dogs returned just after I went back inside the cabin to see to the cats. I couldn't remember the last time I'd been so tired. I wasn't even sure how I'd managed to make it home without falling asleep behind the wheel of my Jeep. I was used to late shifts that ran into the wee hours, but not following two almost sleepless nights. I was tired enough that I was certain I'd fall into a dreamless sleep as soon as my head hit the pillow.

I was wrong.

I lay awake and listened for my captor to return. My breath was shallow, my heart pounding. I knew I needed to make a move or die trying. I clung to the flashlight like a lifeline as I resisted the almost undeniable urge to bring light into my dark, cold world. I knew I needed to wait for the right moment to use both the light and what was left of my strength.

I'd finally figured out who had taken me, although I still didn't understand why. But after what had to have been at least four or five days in this pit, I understood this would end only when I outsmarted my captor or I was dead.

Chapter 7

Thursday, June 21

Houston and I had agreed to meet at the shelter at nine a.m. That gave me a chance to see to my own animals before I left the cabin for the day. I'd called ahead and spoken to the shelter volunteer who'd come in at six to feed the animals, asking him to have Houston wait if he arrived before I did.

As it turned out, we pulled into the parking lot at the same time.

"I can't believe you talked me into this," Houston grumbled good-naturedly.

"I know it's somewhat sudden, especially if you've never considered adopting a dog before, but you're going to love Kojak. Trust me."

"It's odd, but for some reason I do. And that's saying a lot, because I don't trust a lot of people."

"Yeah. Me neither. Most people aren't worthy of trust, but a well-trained dog will never let you down."

In the shelter, I introduced Houston to the volunteers, then gave him a quick tour. Kojak was a large shepherd who'd just turned sixteen months old. He was dropped off six weeks ago by a young couple who'd decided to buy a large dog after moving to Alaska but had never taken the time to train him. Kojak, like a lot of shepherds, had a high-energy level along with a superior intellect. He had so much potential, but he needed a strong owner as well as an active lifestyle and a job to do.

"After Kojak was surrendered to us, I began working with him, as did several of the other volunteers," I said as we walked down the hallway to the pen to which he had been assigned. While most of the dogs were barking as we walked by, Kojak stood at attention and warily watched us approach. "Good morning, Kojak. This is Houston. Houston is a friend." Kojak began to wag his tail. I opened the chain-link gate and clipped a leash onto Kojak's collar. I bent down so he could greet me, then led him into the hallway. "We have an indoor exercise area. I arranged to have it empty so we could work in there."

"He's a beautiful dog. You said he's been here for six weeks. I'm surprised he hasn't been adopted."

"We've had interested parties, but we knew he was going to need a specific sort of human if he was going to reach his true potential, so we waited for the perfect person to come along."

"And you think I'm that perfect person?"

"For Kojak, I do. As I said, he's a very intelligent dog. He's strong and has a high energy level. For him to reach his full potential, he'll need to have a strong handler. An alpha male, if you will."

Houston chuckled. "An alpha male? Now you're just buttering me up for the hard sell."

I grinned and shrugged. "Maybe. Why don't you wait here on the sidelines while I run Kojak through his training exercises? Once I do, you can give it a try."

Houston nodded, then took up a spot next to the wall. At this point we'd trained Kojak to respond with a 90 percent accuracy to the commands Come, Sit, Stay, Heel, Leave It, and Drop. Not every dog could have made the progress he had in such a short amount of time, but there were two men helping with Kojak's training in addition to myself, so most days he was exposed to at least two hours of intensive behavior modification twice a day. Additionally, Kojak wanted to please the humans he'd learned to respect; when we let it be known we were in charge, training went quickly.

"That's really impressive," Houston said.

"Like I said, Kojak is a special dog. I'm going to demonstrate how we pair hand signals with verbal ones. Once you get the idea, I'll have you run Kojak through his routine."

Houston and I worked with Kojak for almost two hours. The man, like the dog, caught on quickly. Houston's large build combined with his deep voice and commanding presence quickly established his role of alpha while working with Kojak. By the end of the session, I could see Houston had not only found a roommate to share his lonely home but, with a little more training, a partner as well.

"So, what do you think?" I asked as the session came to an end.

"Can you teach him to work off lead?"

"Yes. In fact, he's ready to try some off-lead work under highly supervised situations. Usually when we get to this point in his training, I like to take the sessions outdoors. When we have him responding to the basic commands, we can do some testing to see if he's a candidate for specialized training, such as scent tracking, which is useful in search and rescue as well as pursuing and detaining a suspect, and narcotics or bomb detection. Whether he makes the cut in those specialized fields or not, I think he'll be a supportive and loyal companion."

Houston shrugged. "Okay, I'm sold. I'll need supplies. Dog food, a bed. A leash and a collar."

"I can meet you this afternoon to go shopping so you'll have everything you need. As soon as you're set up, I'll come by your place with Kojak. We can show him around his new home together. That way I can ensure that his environment is safe and suited to his needs. You have a fenced yard?"

"I do. I'd like to be able to bring him to work with me as soon as possible, so I'd like to continue with aggressive training."

"We can work out a schedule. Once you have him with you full time, every minute you're together can be a training minute. Maintaining a schedule for specialized training is a good idea, but reinforcing the basics is an ongoing activity. There might be a slight learning curve as the two of you get to know each other, but I think you'll find a comfort zone."

"I get off at five. Can you meet me at the station then?" Houston asked.

"I'll need to check with Jake to make sure I can get the time off, but it shouldn't be a problem. I'll call you later."

After we said good-bye, I returned Kojak to his pen and went back to my place to spend some time working with my own search-and-rescue-dog-in-training. Yukon was doing even better than expected, but I'd need to hone his skills if he was going to end up in the same league as Sitka. Sitka had been trained by a professional dog trainer with a K9 school in Nevada. He came to us ready to work on day one, whereas Yukon was more of a work in progress. I'd just returned from a simulated rescue with Yukon when my phone rang. It was Jake, letting me know we had a real rescue to respond to. I arrived at the trailhead where the team was to meet and be briefed before heading out, and Jake informed me that our missing person—or I guess I should say persons—were Rescue residents Teresa Toller and Diane Fullerton.

According to friends, Diane and Teresa had gone hiking the previous day. Diane was supposed to meet Laura Newberry for dinner that evening but never showed. Laura had tried calling Diane well into the evening and then called Teresa this morning when she still couldn't get hold of her. Teresa likewise didn't answer her phone. When Diane still hadn't returned her calls by lunchtime, Laura called the police. Houston spoke to the neighbors of both Teresa and Diane. No one said they'd seen either of them since the previous week's prayer group, which had been held, I realized with a sinking feeling, at Pastor Brown's church. Houston interviewed the other members of the prayer group, who said Teresa and

Diane had mentioned taking time off from their jobs this Wednesday to hike up to Juniper Falls.

Teresa's car was in her garage, but Diane's was missing. Eventually, it was found at the Juniper Falls trailhead, suggesting the women had set off on the hike as planned but had not returned.

"We're setting off for the falls in two teams," Jake said, after the entire S-and-R team had gathered at the trailhead. "Wyatt, you go with Harmony and Yukon and take grid one." Jake pointed to a rectangle drawn on the map of the area. "I'll take grid two with Sitka and Landon."

"Dani?" I asked.

"She's going to do a sweep of the area with the bird. Austin is going up with her to serve as an extra pair of eyes. Let's do a quick radio check before we start out."

They complied as Jake handed me two plastic bags. One bag had Teresa's clothing, the other Diane's. "If Yukon seems confused by being presented with two different scents, just choose one to give him," he said. "Chances are they're together, so if he finds one, he'll find them both."

"Okay." After everything that had already happened, this rescue had my heart pounding. Would we find the women alive, as we had Silvia, or would we be too late, as we'd been for Pastor Brown? I remembered my dream and my terror was complete.

I started by giving Yukon Teresa's scent. He was so young and had so little S-and-R experience and, as Jake thought it might be, I was afraid that giving him the scents of both women would be confusing. It might have made more sense to give him Diane's scent because it was her car that was found, but

Yukon had met Teresa a few times, and as far as I knew, he'd never had the opportunity to be introduced to Diane.

"This is Teresa. Find Teresa," I said to Yukon.

Wyatt and I set off after Yukon. We put some distance between us to cover more territory, though we'd agreed to maintain sight contact with the others. I think everyone was on edge given the situation. Paying attention to the often very subtle clues left behind by those we sought to find and rescue required a level of concentration I was having a hard time maintaining. I knew what was at stake, so I pushed all other thoughts from my mind and tried to connect with the two women I knew casually.

Teresa was a few years older than me, quiet, and somewhat shy. She worked for the local five-and-dime, and as far as I knew, she was thought to have a pleasant personality. She was tall and thin, with long brown hair she usually wore straight and parted in the middle. Her eyes were brown, her nose pert, and her face narrow. I tried to bring her image into my mind as I followed Yukon who, while progressing steadily toward the falls, had yet to indicate he had picked up on the scent he'd been tasked with following.

Diane was quite a bit older than Teresa, maybe in her midfifties, but she was in good shape, outgoing, and extroverted. She worked as a teacher at the local school. She was short and carried a few extra pounds, although most considered her attractive. She had shoulder-length blond hair I was pretty sure she bleached. She had green eyes, a round face, and a welcoming smile that drew you in.

As I had with Teresa, I brought Diane's image to mind and tried to focus on it. So far, I wasn't picking up either woman, and that scared me. Usually, if I was unable to hone in on the subject of one of our searches, it was for one of three reasons. The most common was that the person wasn't actually in need of rescuing. We received many calls from concerned parents and spouses who jumped the gun and reported their loved one missing when they'd simply lost track of time and were late getting home.

The second most common reason I was unable to connect with the subject of a search was because they were already dead. My gift was to connect psychically with those I was meant to save. If they were already dead, there was no one to connect to.

The third and final reason I might not be able to connect with the victim of a search was if they were, for some reason, blocking me. It hadn't happened often because most of the time, victims weren't even aware I was poking around in their heads, but it had occurred a time or two, so I knew it was possible.

In this case, I suspected reason two but hoped for reason one. Normally, I wouldn't jump to the conclusion that someone was dead, but after the horrific dreams I'd been having, I probably had death on my mind.

"Sitka has something," Jake said over the radio.

"Copy," I responded. "Do you want us to change course?"

"Negative," Jake answered. "Keep to your current route for now, but let me know if Yukon alerts. Did you give him both scents?"

"No. Just Teresa's."

"Okay, that's fine. Giving him a single scent is probably the best move. Sitka is heading in your direction. We'll see where he leads."

By the time Sitka had led Jake and Landon to a location that intersected with the trail Wyatt and I were following, I could hear the falls in the distance. I'd seen Dani and Austin fly overhead a few times as we made the trek up the mountain, but the last time she'd reported in they hadn't seen a sign of either woman.

"Let's take a minute to regroup," Jake suggested after his search party merged with mine. "Harmony, I want you to sit down and relax. Don't worry about Yukon or any of us. Just focus on the women and see if you can connect to either of them."

I did as Jake asked. I decided to focus on the women one at a time. I started with Diane. I brought her face into view. I tried to see where she might be or what she might be doing, but I didn't get a thing. After a few minutes I changed direction and focused on Teresa. I was still coming up empty. I worked harder, and this time I felt a whisper of emotion. Fear. There was a hint of pain, a hint of darkness, and then nothing.

"Anything?" Jake asked when I opened my eyes.

"I'm not picking up Diane at all. Not even a blip on the screen. In my opinion, she's either not in pain or danger and therefore not in need of rescue, or she's dead."

"Any guess as to which?" Jake's mouth hardened.

"If she was injured or frightened, I'm sure I'd be picking up *something*. Even when we were looking for Vinnie the other day, before he realized he was lost, I was able to pick up a vague feeling of curiosity. With Diane, there's nothing. I'm really afraid she might be dead."

Jake took a breath, then asked about Teresa.

"I can't see her, and the connection isn't strong. I'm not even a hundred percent certain I'm getting a connection at all. But when I focus on her, I pick up fear. I also feel I can sense darkness and pain. But the connection fades in and out. For all I know, there could be someone else in the area in need of help and I'm picking up their energy, not Teresa's."

"You're thinking you're connecting with the woman in your dreams?"

"Maybe. It feels like the image I have in my head could be her. I know Teresa, and I'm not getting a strong sense she's the one my mind is trying to connect with."

Jake sighed. "I guess it's up to the dogs. I gave both scents to Sitka, so I'm not sure which woman he's been tracking, but he seems to be tracking someone. I'll give him both scents again and we'll follow."

"Should I give Yukon either scent?" I asked. "I gave him Teresa before, but he never demonstrated he'd picked up the scent."

"Give him both scents," Jake said. "It might confuse him, but it might not."

Jake, Landon, Wyatt, and I spread out as we followed Sitka, who seemed to know exactly where he wanted to go. Yukon stuck with Sitka, and while I didn't know whether he'd picked anything up or was simply mimicking his mentor and buddy, he too began to alert now that he had both scents. Maybe it was Diane the dogs were tracking.

"Dani to Jake, do you copy?" I heard her voice over the radio we all carried.

"I copy. Do you have something?" Jake answered.

"Maybe. Austin can see what looks to be a jacket downriver from the falls. It's red. There are trees in the area, so we can't get a very good look, but it doesn't appear there's a body to go with it. Still, you might want to check it out. With all the trees, it's impossible to know for sure."

"We're on it." Jake paused for just a few seconds and then said to us, "Landon and I will continue to follow Sitka, who appears to be heading to the top of the falls. Harmony and Wyatt, take Yukon and go for the coordinates Dani is providing. Once you locate the object Austin is getting a peek at from the sky, radio and let us know what you're looking at."

"Ten-four," I answered.

Dani called in the coordinates and Wyatt took out his compass to set a course. She'd indicated we were a half mile out, which in this terrain was likely to take a good twenty minutes to traverse. The red object that appeared to be a jacket was, thankfully, on our side of the river. With the annual runoff in full force, there was no way we'd be able to cross it.

"Something on your mind?" Wyatt asked after we'd been hiking to the river for about ten minutes. "Besides the obvious, that is."

I glanced at him but kept walking as briskly as the terrain would allow. "There's something off about this. I can't quite put my finger on it, but I have a bad feeling about things."

"Because you haven't been able to make a connection?"

"Yes, partially. But also because when I did sense something earlier, it was fragmented. I don't think the fear and pain I picked up were coming from either Diane or Teresa."

"So, you think there's a third victim?"

I paused before I answered. I wished I felt more certain about things. "I don't know. Maybe. I've been having dreams about a woman who's being held in a cold, dark place. It could be just a dream, but I feel like it might be more. I don't have enough evidence either way. I guess all we can do is find the women we have been tasked to rescue, then see how it all works out."

"Did you tell Jake about your dreams?"

I nodded. "Last night. We discussed the various things it could mean, but that's all we could do at this point."

As we neared the roaring river, I put Yukon on the lead. I hoped he'd be smart enough not to venture into the water, but better to be safe than sorry. After we exited the tree cover and entered the large clearing Dani had indicated was to the north of the jacket, we went south, paralleling the quickly flowing water. Shortly after we reentered the trees, we spotted the jacket. Just as Dani said, it was laying at the water's edge.

"Wyatt to Jake," Wyatt said into the radio. "We have the jacket. So far, there's no sign of the jacket's owner. We'll look around a bit to see what we can find."

"Chances are the jacket belongs to a hiker or rafter who lost it somewhere upstream," I said. "The river widens here, and there are a lot of rocks around. I'm willing to bet the jacket became snagged on a rock, or maybe a tree branch, then ended up in the shallower water that eventually led to it getting tangled up on the shore."

Wyatt walked up and down the waterline, looking for additional debris. "Yeah. I don't see anything."

I picked up the wet jacket, holding it away from my body to avoid becoming soaked by it. I tried to hone in on its owner but wasn't getting anything. I put my hand into the pocket and was immediately overcome with a feeling of terror I had to struggle to control.

"What is it?" Wyatt asked.

"Terror. Cold. Darkness." I gasped as I tried to slow my breathing. "Hopelessness."

"Can you see who? Or where?"

I shook my head. "No. It's quiet. I don't hear the water, so I don't think it's nearby."

"Do you think you're picking up on the owner of the jacket?"

"No. Not the jacket." I held out a necklace. The thin gold chain was broken, but the solitary diamond in the center of a gold heart was intact. "This."

Wyatt looked at it and frowned. "So you're picking up on the owner of the necklace, not the jacket. Does that mean they belong to different people?"

I closed my hand over the necklace again. "I'm not getting anything from the jacket, but the necklace is special to the person who owns it. I don't know who owns the jacket or how the necklace came to be in its pocket, but the owner of the necklace is in trouble."

"What kind of trouble?" Wyatt asked.

"I don't know. It's dark and cold. Maybe a cave. But not here. I don't sense that she's here by the river or even at the falls." I opened my eyes. "I think this necklace belongs to the person in my dreams."

"Jake to team two." The radio on my belt crackled while Wyatt and I were discussing the necklace.

"Go ahead," Wyatt said into his radio.

"We found Diane."

"She's dead," I whispered before Jake confirmed what I knew to be true.

"How long?" Wyatt asked.

"Not more than a few hours. We're at the top of the falls. I don't have cell reception, so Dani will need to contact Officer Houston."

"I'm on it," Dani confirmed and then rang off.

"Any sign of Teresa?" I asked as regret for a life cut short settled into my heart.

"No," Jake answered. "Landon is going to wait here for Officer Houston. I'm giving Sitka Teresa's scent. Do the same with Yukon. I know he wasn't picking it up before, but I don't see how we can leave until we know for sure."

I looked toward the sun, which wouldn't set for hours. At least we didn't have to worry about getting caught in the dark. "Okay," I answered. "Harmony out."

I didn't have a lot of faith that Yukon would be any better able to pick up Teresa's scent now than he had before, but if she was out here, Sitka would find her. He always found his target if it was there to find.

Chapter 8

Later, at the debriefing, we learned Diane's throat had been slit, the same as Pastor Brown's. And, like Pastor Brown, it was determined she most likely died slowly. Her clothing too was wet, but she hadn't been left in the water to die.

While we'd been looking for Diane, Houston had been able to track down Teresa at her sister's. She told him she'd planned to go hiking too, but Diane had canceled at the last minute, so she'd gone to Fairbanks to spend a couple of days there. Her sister had picked her up early on Tuesday morning. Teresa didn't know why Diane would have gone ahead with the hike after canceling with her, and she agreed with my assessment that Diane wouldn't have tackled the hike alone. According to Houston, Diane had been dead long before I tried to connect with her on Wednesday afternoon. I was pretty sure none of the flashes I'd been getting were linked to her.

A chill worked its way up my spine as I reached into my pocket and grasped the necklace I'd found in the pocket of the red jacket. I probably should have given it to Houston along with the jacket, but I had the feeling it could be the key to identifying the person I'd sensed but had been unable to really connect with.

It was after five by the time I got home from the rescue, so it was too late to go dog supply shopping with Houston. I called to reschedule, and when I did, he'd said he had something to talk to me about. He asked if it would be okay if he brought takeout over to my place. I was exhausted, but I was curious to hear what was on his mind, so I agreed. I had time to take the dogs for a quick walk and then feed everyone. I had just finished cleaning the cat boxes when my doggy alarm system went off and a chorus of barks alerted me that Houston had arrived.

"Relax," I said before opening the door. I eyed each dog as they obediently sat and waited for me to answer the knock.

"That's quite an alarm system you have," Houston greeted.

"It's the best kind. Come on in." I stood aside.

Houston eyed the dogs warily as he tentatively took a step into the cabin. He glanced at each dog in turn, settling on Denali, who was sitting quietly, as he'd been told to do, though he hadn't quite quelled the deep growls coming from his chest. "Are you sure it's okay?"

"It's fine. They've been told to stand down. They'll do as they're told." Once Houston, who was dressed casually in jeans and a sweatshirt, was completely inside, I introduced him to the family who, except for the always-on-guard Denali, began to wag their tails, accepting him as a new friend who'd come to play. "Why don't we dig into whatever smells so good before it gets cold? You can fill me in on whatever you wanted to talk about while we eat."

"Fine by me. I'm starving."

We divided up the cheesy pasta dish Houston had picked up at Neverland and we took seats at my small dining table. Then he slid a photo across the table. It was a man in his forties with light hair cropped military style. Gray eyes and chiseled features devoid of even the slightest warmth or animation seemed to demonstrate that he was a serious man with a singular purpose that wouldn't be denied. A chill crept up my spine as I continued to study that face. "Who is he?"

"His name is Damian Ragland. After you told me the man who'd picked up Silvia had been driving an Avis rental, I began my search for a male who'd picked up a dark blue Ford Focus in the days preceding Silvia's abduction. Apparently, it's a popular rental car; the list was longer than I'd anticipated. I was, however, able to narrow things down quite a bit when I took in to account that the man had most likely been alone and would probably have already turned in the vehicle. Eventually, I came up with this man."

I looked at the photo again. "Why would he kidnap Silvia?"

"I'm still not certain of all the details, but I'm beginning to put together a profile. It seems he was born right here in Rescue to Todd and Betty Ragland. Betty passed away after a short illness when Damian was nine. Her husband was a rugged outdoorsman, but, based on a police report I was able to dig up, had no idea how to raise a child. He was a hard and rigid man who went from ignoring the child to taking out his frustrations on him. When Damian was twelve, one of his teachers noticed bruises on his arms, legs, and torso, which she reported to the police. The officer on duty spoke to the boy's father, but that only seemed to make him angrier. The beatings became more frequent and severe. The court ordered counseling services for both father and son, but it didn't seem to make much of a difference in their relationship. When Damian was thirteen he was taken from his father and sent to live with an uncle in Anchorage. From what I've been able to uncover, Ragland was a difficult child who had trouble fitting in with a traditional family. Eventually he was removed from his uncle's home and put into the foster care system. He was too angry and too aggressive to find a placement with one of the foster families in the area, so he spent most of his teens in group homes. When he was eighteen, he joined the Army, where he seemed to thrive and was recruited by Special Forces. Ragland was good with a gun and didn't mind using it, which served him well over the course of his career. By the time the war in Afghanistan rolled around, he was a highly decorated sniper."

"What does Silvia have to do with any of this?" I asked.

"Hang on; I'm getting to that. In 2008, Ragland was involved in an ill-fated mission that resulted in civilian casualties. His entire team was subjected to an in-depth review to determine whether there had been negligence involved in what can only be described as a tragic error. While Ragland was never brought up on official charges—due, I believe, to a lack of conclusive evidence—it's my opinion, based on what I've been able to find out, and the opinion of others who looked into the case, that it was his decision to act outside of the designated plan that led to the rampage that resulted in the civilian deaths. In the end, it was Ragland's choice to leave the Army. After he was discharged, he simply disappeared, and to the extent that any man is able to, became a ghost."

"What do you mean by ghost?" I asked.

"Basically, that while he seems to make a living as a hitman, he never stays in one place for long, which has made him impossible to track down."

I took a deep breath and let Houston's words sink in. "Okay, this is a very tragic story, but why would you think he kidnapped Silvia?"

"I not only think Ragland kidnapped Silvia, I think he's responsible for both Pastor Brown and Diane's murders as well."

I'd had a feeling the three deaths would come down to a single perpetrator. "Say you're right. Why these three individuals?"

"They were all connected to Ragland and, in some way, contributed to his being removed from his home when he was a teen. Diane Fullerton was the teacher who called law enforcement when she noticed he had extensive bruises on his body. Pastor Brown knew the family and the situation and tried to intervene. He tried mentoring him but ultimately testified against Damian's father at the custody hearing. I can see how he would feel betrayed by this."

"And Silvia?"

"Silvia White was the doctor who saw him after his teacher noticed his injuries. She also testified at the hearing that resulted in his removal from his father's home."

"You think this man has come home after all these years to punish the people who took him from his father?"

Houston nodded.

"But why? If a child is being beaten by his father, you'd think he'd be glad to be removed from the home."

"In my experience, as illogical as it may seem, many children have deep affection for their abusive parents. At times, the violence serves to deepen the bond beyond that of a normal parent-child relationship. Additionally, Ragland was tossed from the pot into the fire. From what I can tell, his life became a hell on earth after the removal. I have no doubt the people who worked to have him removed from his father's care had the best of intentions. Unfortunately, their actions only ended up making things worse for him."

I sat back in my chair. Suddenly, my appetite was nonexistent. "Okay, say Damian Ragland is the one who killed Pastor Brown and Diane Fullerton and intended to kill Silvia White. Why now? He has to be, what, forty?"

"Forty-two. I'm not sure why he decided now was the time for him to right what he probably perceived to be a great wrong. I'm going to assume something occurred to set him off. His actions here seem to have been carefully planned and executed."

The more I thought about it, the more Houston's theory fit. Pastor Brown had told Jolene he couldn't stay to watch a movie with the family because he was meeting an old acquaintance. Silvia took a last-minute ride with an old friend. And Diane canceled her plans to go hiking with Teresa at the last minute. Most likely Ragland had contacted her, asking to meet. "Is that all?" I asked. "Are there others?"

"I'm afraid there might be." Houston took a piece of paper from the folder he'd been carrying when he'd arrived. I hadn't noticed it until after he sat down and began to speak. "After I discovered Ragland was our suspect, I made a list of everyone who'd been involved in the hearing that resulted in his being removed from his father's home. Diane Fullerton was the teacher who saw his extensive bruises and went to the police. Phillip Osgood was the officer who first responded to her complaint. He had Ragland checked out by a doctor, Silvia White. She reported that he had not only suffered a recent beating but there was evidence of broken bones and extensive scarring going back years. Both Ragland and his father were required to undergo counseling. The counselor they were assigned to was Jennifer Walton, who was unable to do much to change the dad's outlook on life, but she saw promise in the boy and enlisted the help of Pastor Brown. She felt Ragland would benefit from having a positive male role model and hoped the pastor would fill that role. When things continued to escalate at home, Walton recommended to the court that Ragland be removed. All the people mentioned testified at the hearing that was arranged. Judge Frank Noltie transferred the boy's custody to his uncle, who eventually claimed he was unable to meet the needs of the rebellious teen. Ragland was then placed in foster care and lived out his adolescence in a group home."

"Diane and Pastor Brown are dead, and Dr. White is in the hospital. Do you know what became of Walton, Officer Osgood, and Judge Noltie?"

"Officer Osgood is retired and living in Florida. Judge Noltie died after suffering a heart attack eight years ago. Jennifer Walton lives in Fairbanks. Her husband reported her missing last Saturday. Apparently, she received a phone call at around eleven a.m. and told her husband she needed to run out to meet an old client but wouldn't be more than a couple of hours. When she hadn't returned by eight that night, he called the police. I was able to determine that Ragland arrived in Fairbanks and rented the Ford on Friday evening. It seems likely he arrived in Rescue to meet with Father Brown by midday on Sunday. I don't know for certain Ragland abducted Walton, but I have good reason to suspect he did. What I don't know is whether she's still alive. As best I can tell, it's Ragland's MO to kidnap his victims, hold them overnight, and then kill them the following day."

My heart was pounding, my palms sweaty. I had a million questions I felt needed to be asked, but my mouth was so dry I couldn't speak. I reached for my water glass and took a long swallow. It did seem like Ragland was following a pattern. Pastor Brown was meeting him on Sunday evening. It was most likely he was abducted then, and the ME believed he died on Monday morning. Silvia was abducted and left in the cave on Tuesday. It seemed reasonable to assume Ragland planned to come back to kill her on Wednesday, but we found her before he was able to do it. Diane was kidnapped on Wednesday. While I didn't know what would be in the ME's official report, we'd already assumed she'd been killed this morning. Given the pattern, if Jennifer Walton had been abducted on Saturday, she would have been killed on Sunday, but I had a feeling she was still alive.

"Do you have a photo of Jennifer Walton?" I asked.

Houston slid one across the table to me. Dark hair. Dark eyes. Somehow, I knew she was the woman in my dreams. "I think I've been connecting with her for days. I just didn't know it was her. We have to find her."

"Any idea where to start?" Houston asked.

My mind was racing, which would only hinder my ability to focus and make a connection. "I need to get something from my room. Call Jake. Tell him to come over. Tell him to put the rest of the team on alert."

I ran into my room and grabbed the necklace I'd found. I returned to the living room, sat down on the sofa, and clutched it in my hand as I tried to pull up an image of the woman in my mind. Nice smile. Dark, warm eyes. Thick dark hair that flowed over her shoulders. Initially, she'd seemed so weak. I'd felt the woman in my dreams was close to death, but with every day that passed it seemed she grew stronger. More determined. I remembered her thinking she would need to make a move. Try to escape. I wondered if she had. I wondered if her valiant efforts had gotten her killed.

I could hear Houston in the distance, on the phone. I tried to ignore him, but I was having a hard time focusing as I needed to. I was about to ask him to take his call outside when I heard him sign off. I listened as he came into the living room and sat down on the chair across from me. He didn't say anything, for which I was grateful.

"The jacket we found during our search for Diane," I began. "Were you ever able to determine where it had come from or who it belonged to?"

Houston looked confused. "Is that relevant to this situation?"

I showed him the necklace. "I found this in the pocket. I think it belongs to the woman I've been connecting with."

"I haven't been able to confirm whose it is, but I heard there was a group of visitors from Fairbanks who were brought here by a charter company to do some white-water rafting. They were making their way down the river upstream from the falls when they capsized. I suspect the jacket may belong to one of them."

"We need to find out for sure. If this necklace does belong to the woman I've been dreaming of, whoever owned the jacket may have information that can help us find her."

"I'll have one of my men track down the owner of the tour company. Maybe he'll know who lost the jacket."

Houston got up to make his call and I began to rub the necklace between my fingers. I cleared my mind and concentrated with everything I had. Up until this point, I hadn't been sure if my dream had been a vision, but after seeing the photo of Jennifer Walton, I was certain she was the person who'd been spending time in my head.

After I'd been meditating for a good ten minutes, an image began to take shape. Trees, bright light, the sound of birds overhead. She was no longer in the dark place where she'd been held all week but outside somewhere, amid the forest, the birds, and the healing sunshine. My first instinct was that she'd carried through with the last thought she'd had before our connection had been broken the previous night. The thought to take a stand and fight for her life instead of giving in to the darkness. But then I felt a pain. A sharp, searing pain. I gasped.

"Are you okay?" Houston asked as he came back into the room.

"I'm fine," I answered without opening my eyes. "It's not my pain I feel but hers."

"So she's still alive?"

I nodded "For now." I took a deep breath in and slowly let it out. "I sense she's outdoors. In the forest, not in the dark place where I'd been sensing her all week. Her feet are bare, her hands bound with a rough, sturdy rope that has scraped the skin from her wrists. She has a gash on her forehead, but otherwise she seems unharmed except for deep cuts on her feet. She has tape over her mouth, but she feels strong and determined. She hasn't given in. I wouldn't either."

I opened my eyes.

"Do you know where she is?"

I shook my head. "I just see forest. She's walking. I sense her captor is with her, but I don't see him. He may be walking behind her. Did you get any information on the jacket?"

"It belonged to one of the men on the rafting trip. I asked him about the necklace and he said he found it on the sidewalk outside a Starbucks in Fairbanks. He picked it up and meant to turn it in at the police station because he thought it might be valuable, but he got caught up in getting to the group for the rafting trip and forgot all about it."

"Jennifer Walton lives in Fairbanks, so that could fit. Still, the odds that he'd pick it up in the city and I'd find it in Rescue must be pretty huge. Add to that the fact that I've been dreaming about her for days and they're astronomical."

"Or the whole thing was meant to be."

"Yeah. I guess there's that."

The dogs all jumped up as Jake walked in through the cabin door. He greeted them, then sat down beside me. "What do we have?" he asked.

"The woman I dreamed about is no longer in the dark place she'd been kept all week," I said, then told him everything I knew.

"Do you have any idea where she is?" Jake asked.

I furrowed my brow. "No. At least not yet. All I can see are trees and a little bit of sky. It could be anywhere. Houston can tell you anything you don't already know. I need to try to reconnect."

I closed my eyes again and willed myself to relax. I envisioned Jennifer Walton's face, biting my lip. I needed to resist the urge to start chasing every thought that stomped its way through my mind. I took a moment to consider the larger picture, then choose the best place to begin our search. Jennifer's life most likely depended on it.

I opened my eyes and looked at Jake. "The locations Ragland has chosen to hide and kill his victims feel specific to me. It appears he kidnaps his victim the day before he plans to kill them, leaves them bound and gagged, then makes them walk to their death. It feels like the pattern has a very intentional purpose."

"Perhaps by making them wait for death he's giving them time to suffer," Jake suggested.

"Or perhaps he's giving them time to repent."

"Repent?" Houston said. "Why do they need to repent? He's the one killing people."

"Maybe Ragland believes the people responsible for the hell he endured after being taken from his father are guilty of some sort of sin. Maybe something as simple as *honor thy father*, but it could be something else. These people have done wrong in his eyes, and the cost of doing wrong is death."

"So he's both the judge handing down the sentence he feels is justified and the executioner?" Jake said.

"Yeah, it could be something like that. I'm only imagining what he might be feeling, though I'm sure I picked up some of his thoughts during Vinnie's rescue." I turned back to Houston. "Where did Jennifer meet Ragland and his father when she counseled them after it was determined the father had been abusive?"

"I'm not sure."

"Was it their home? Her home? Did she have an office? Did they meet at the school? The church?"

"Does it matter?" Jake asked.

I nodded. "I think it does. The locations in which Ragland has killed his victims seem specific. I bet if you do a little digging, you'll find Pastor Brown took young Damian fishing at Glacier Lake while doing the male-bonding thing. We don't know where Dr. White would have been killed if things had gone according to plan, but I bet we would have found her body near the clinic where Damian was treated. And Diane was found at the top of Juniper Falls. She took her entire class hiking up to the falls every year when the water was low. There's that little pool you can swim in if it's warm enough. I'm guessing it was while Damian was swimming in that pool that Diane noticed his cuts and bruises."

"That makes a lot of sense," Houston said. "And if you're right, Ragland plans to kill Jennifer at or near wherever the counseling sessions were held." Houston stood up. "I need to make a call. Keep working. I'll take it outside."

I closed my eyes and again tried to focus in on Jennifer. I needed to see what she saw, hear what she heard, feel what she felt. She'd lived in Rescue before moving to Fairbanks. At some point she'd realize where they were, and the location would cross her mind.

"Jennifer didn't have an office," I heard Houston say when he returned to the room. "The woman I spoke to said her clients would go to her home to meet. When she met with parents, she would go to them. I have my team tracking down where she and the Raglands lived."

"I'll have the team stand by. They'll be ready to move out within a moment's notice," Jake said.

I opened my eyes. "They're at a pool of water. Ragland is submerging Jennifer."

"He's going to drown her?" Jake asked.

"No. Not drown. He's cleansing her, maybe baptizing her."

"Both Pastor Brown and Diane were near water when we found them," Jake said. "And they were both wet."

"Do you recognize the pool?" Houston asked.

I closed my eyes and focused. I gasped, and my eyes shot open. "They're here. At the little pond in the forest a quarter mile or so beyond the boundary of my property. There's a cabin there. It's been deserted since I've lived here, but I know it was occupied at one time."

Houston took his gun out of his holster, then used a radio to call his own team. He looked at Jake. "Have your people stand down. This isn't a rescue. It might very well turn into a hostage situation. I don't want anyone getting hurt."

"I'll have the team stand down, but I'm coming with you. I have a rifle in my truck."

"I'm coming too," I said as I grabbed my own rifle from its hanger on the wall near the door. I could see both men were about to argue. "Nonnegotiable," I said as I told the dogs to stay, then headed out into the light of a northern Alaska summer.

Jake and Houston fell in beside me. I knew exactly where I was going and they didn't, so neither of them argued when I took the lead. When we were a hundred yards or so from the cabin I paused and crouched down behind some shrubs.

"The pond is about an eighth of a mile through those trees. Jennifer is coming through strongly now. She's okay, but Ragland has her on her knees. He's talking to her. Ranting, really." I paused and focused. "They're walking again. I can't tell in which direction."

"Let's move," Houston said.

This time, he took the lead, while Jake and I followed behind. When we arrived at the pond, there was evidence someone had been there, but the place was deserted.

"Any idea where they went?" Houston asked.

"Give me a minute." I closed my eyes, waiting for Jennifer's image to appear in my head. I gasped. "They must have doubled back around somehow. They're heading back to the cabin."

"We need to get back before he kills her," Houston said.

We all took off running. As we approached the cabin, we slowed our pace. Taking positions behind trees, we watched as Ragland stood with Jennifer on the deck. He made her get to her knees again and took a knife from his belt.

"He's going to kill her now," I whispered.

Houston took a step into the clearing. "Drop the knife!" he yelled, pointing his revolver at Ragland, who grabbed Jennifer and pulled her to her feet. He used her as a shield as he backed to the door. He pulled the door open and they disappeared inside.

"We need to get her," I said.

"It'd be better to wait for my men."

"But he might kill her before they get here," I argued.

Jennifer appeared at the window at the front of the cabin. She stood perfectly still. We waited for her to make a move of some sort, but she just stood there, looking out.

"Why is she just standing there?" I asked.

Houston frowned. "I don't know, but I don't like it. I say we go in after all."

"I'll circle around through the forest to the right. Jake, you circle around to the left. We'll approach the front door from either side to reduce the chance of us being seen. Harmony, you stay here. If things go south, you're our only backup."

I nodded. "Okay, but hurry. This doesn't feel right."

They disappeared into the trees. I held my breath, trying to reconnect with Jennifer. Her mind was perfectly calm and still. It didn't make sense, and I certainly didn't understand why she was just standing there. I could feel Houston and Jake moving through the forest. I didn't know how this would go, but I was terrified it would end badly.

I held my breath, then, as Jake and Houston reappeared, approaching the door from opposite sides. On Houston's signal, they stormed the door. I watched as Houston approached Jennifer. She was still standing perfectly still, but he was talking to her. As I stood there, unable to understand what was going on, Houston's men arrived. They went in immediately, and Jake came out to me.

"What's going on?" I demanded. "Why is Jennifer just standing there? Where's Ragland?"

"He's gone. Apparently, there's a trapdoor that leads to an underground passage. It looks old. It probably was there when he was a child. This was their home."

"And Jennifer?"

"Ragland attached something to her. He told her it was a bomb, and it would go off if she moved, but Houston doesn't think it would have. It's amateur stuff he thinks he can defuse, but he has the bomb squad on the phone."

"Shouldn't we be doing something?" I asked.

"Houston said to wait outside, so I say we wait. It's not like either of us can help with this."

Jake had a point, but I wasn't sure how I'd be able to stand around doing nothing while I waited to find out if the person I'd been carrying around in my head all week went home to her husband or died in a fiery explosion.

Chapter 9

Friday, June 22

"So Ragland used Jennifer and the bomb as a diversion while he got away?" Chloe said the next morning as we drank coffee at her café.

"Unfortunately, yes."

"Do they have any leads on him? Do they think he's still in this area? Will he be looking for more victims?"

"There are no leads at this point as far as I know, and they don't know if he's left here or is still lurking about. I'd think if he's still in this area, he'll lay low rather than looking for additional victims now that he knows the police are on to him, but I really have no idea."

"You should be careful," Chloe said. "I mean extremely, compulsively careful. I wouldn't be surprised if he isn't going to come after you next.

You're the reason his plans for Silvia and Jennifer were foiled. If he's as smart as it sounds, he must have figured that out by now."

I frowned. "I guess it wouldn't hurt to sleep with my rifle for a few days."

"A rifle won't do you a lot of good if he has a bomb," Chloe pointed out. "Why did he have a bomb anyway? Did he just have one laying around in case he needed to create a diversion, or did he plan to do something with it?"

"That's a really good question. Why *did* he have a bomb? Once Jake, Houston, and I showed up, everything went really quickly. Ragland pulled Jennifer into the cabin and tied the bomb to her, saying it would go off if she moved. He used the time Houston spent dealing with the fact that Ragland was holding her hostage and trying to figure out how to disarm the bomb to get away. He slit the throats of his other victims. At least the ones I know about. A bomb, even a small, homemade one like that, is a whole new element."

After I left Chloe's I headed to the shelter. Houston was supposed to meet me there for our delayed shopping trip and training session. I wasn't sure he'd show, considering everything else he had on his plate, but when I pulled into the parking lot his truck was already there.

"Are you ready to be a daddy?" I greeted Houston, who'd been chatting with Serena.

"A daddy?"

I had to laugh. "Getting a dog is a bit like having a baby. A dog will bring a lot of love into your life, but it also impacts your usual routine. Of course, Kojak is doing well with his training and is fairly self-sufficient, so the learning curve shouldn't be too bad. Let's grab a leash and take your new baby shopping."

"The dog is coming with us?"

"Absolutely. It's a good idea to expose Kojak to as many different experiences as you can. You want first and foremost to be sure he's well socialized. The pet store where we're going to get the supplies you need allows dogs, so we may as well bring him along."

I grabbed a leash and the dog, and we went out to Houston's truck. I gave him directions to the only pet supply store in town.

"Any news about Ragland?" I asked as we pulled onto the highway.

"Not so far. We have an APB out on him; he won't get far."

"You think he's left town?"

"Makes sense he would. He knows we're on to him and that we know who he is and what he looks like. He'd be pretty stupid to stay nearby."

"What if he isn't done? What if Jennifer wasn't the last victim?"

Houston turned and looked at me. "Do you have another victim in mind? Are you sensing something?"

"No," I said. "I'm just making conversation. Have you spoken to Jennifer?"

Houston nodded. "She's home now. She was checked out at the hospital in Fairbanks, but they didn't keep her because her injuries weren't life-threatening. She confirmed a lot of what we already knew. She said she received a call from Ragland wanting to meet her for coffee. He told her that he was back in the States after a career in the military and wanted to take the opportunity to ask her a few questions about his childhood. Normally, she wouldn't agree to meet a client, or even an ex-client, outside of office hours, but he said he was only in Alaska for the weekend, so she agreed to meet him at Starbucks. When she arrived, he came up from behind her and pricked her with something. It immediately made her dizzy and she passed out shortly after, but she remembers being helped into a car. The next thing she knew, she was laying on a cold floor in a room so dark she couldn't make out a single thing."

"She must have been terrified."

"I'm sure she was," Houston agreed. "She didn't know how long she'd been out when she finally came to and had no way of knowing how long she was in the room before Ragland came for her."

"In my dream, at some point he gave her water, a loaf of bread, and a flashlight."

"She confirmed that did occur. She rationed the food and the flashlight batteries. At one point he tossed an old mattress into the room for her to lay on."

"That demonstrates compassion," I said. "It didn't seem he was the sort to possess an ounce of compassion. I suppose the mattress was some kind of indicator that she was different to him than the others. I wonder if he planned to keep her longer when he first took her or if he changed his mind about killing her right away after he got her here."

"I doubt we'll ever know unless he volunteers the information when we catch him," Houston said. "Based on what I've learned about him, he doesn't seem like the sort to want to talk about his feelings."

"The room where Jennifer was kept—was it located in the underground passage beneath the cabin?"

"Yes. My men and I looked after we diffused the bomb. There's a small room with a door that locks from the outside about halfway along the passage. Really more like a closet."

"If the passage and the room were there already when Ragland lived there with his father, it makes me think he might have been locked in that room himself."

Houston frowned. "I hadn't thought of that, but it does seem like a possibility. It would also explain why Ragland kept his victims in cold, dark places before he killed them."

I know I shouldn't feel compassion for a killer, but somehow, I did. The poor kid; no wonder he'd turned out the way he had. If Jennifer hadn't regained consciousness until after she was locked in the dark room, that explained why she didn't know where she was being held, though I was surprised she hadn't recognized the cabin when Ragland brought her out of the room to go to the pond. Of course, he may have taken her through the passage and out the back way, which most likely opened somewhere in the forest.

"Did Jennifer say what was going on at the pond?" I asked as we pulled into the parking lot of the pet store.

"He forced her under the water several times while he shouted at her, but she said the words didn't make sense. She thought he was planning to drown her, but then he grabbed her by the hair and told her to walk back the way they'd come. When they got back to the cabin, he pulled out a knife. She was sure he planned to end her life with it. If we'd arrived even a minute later, she probably would be dead."

"Well, it's a good thing we showed up when we did. Why don't you park near the door? We're going to have a lot of things to load when we're done."

Before we got out, I clicked the leash on Kojak. Then Houston lowered the tailgate, allowing the dog to jump down. He seemed excited to be going on an adventure. I just hoped he'd behave, so Houston wouldn't change his mind about the adoption before he even got him home.

******

"Which toy?" Houston held a stuffed doggy in one hand and a stuffed moose in the other. Kojak was sitting in front of him, looking intently at the offerings. After a few seconds, Kojak had lifted his front paw and touched the moose. Houston tossed it into the basket. So far, Houston had allowed Kojak to pick his own bed, collar, leash, chew toy, sleeping toy, and dog biscuits. I suggested he just buy the food that was best suited for a dog of Kojak's size, rather than letting him choose his own. From the conversation that seemed to be going on between the man and his new best friend, breakfast was going to consist of Froot Loops for both dog and man, so a nutritious dinner was going to be a must.

After we'd filled two baskets with everything any dog could want or need, and more toys than one dog could reasonably play with, we headed to Houston's house. I wasn't sure what I was expecting, but certainly not the two-story structure perched on the bank of the lake. It was on a large lot, a portion of which was fenced, providing plenty of room for Kojak to get as much exercise as he desired.

"You have a beautiful piece of property," I said as Houston pulled into the circular drive.

"I like it. When I came to Rescue to officially accept the job and find a place to live, this was the first place the real estate agent showed me. I fell in love with it and bought it without looking at anything else."

I opened the truck door and stepped out. Across the lake was a gorgeous view of the mountains. I bet it was lovely in the morning as the sun came up. I could picture Houston sitting on the wraparound deck, drinking his coffee and welcoming the day.

Houston lowered the tailgate and Kojak jumped down. He ran around, sniffing everything in sight but not wandering too far. He'd come so far with his training in such a short time. I really did have high hopes for him.

I helped Houston carry everything inside, then let him give me a tour before we went back outside for a short training session. We'd gone through the basics and were working on retrieval exercises when I got a call from Kelly. The moose was doing better, and she hoped I'd be able to take him home for the weekend. I promised to be by to get him before she closed for the day.

"What was that all about?" Houston asked, as Kojak politely dropped the hard rubber object shaped like a stick we used for training at his feet.

"It was Kelly, the local veterinarian. You should meet her. She was calling to ask if I could pick up my moose today."

"Your moose?"

"A baby moose. Less than a week old. Abandoned, with a broken leg. He's going to hang out in my barn with Homer until we can come up with a long-term plan for him."

"Homer?"

"My blind mule. I guess I didn't have time to introduce you when you came by. Anyway, I told Kelly I'd be by before she closes. If you can drive me back to my Jeep, that would be great."

Houston glanced at me with a look of amazement on his face. "You want me to take you back to your Jeep so you can pick up your moose and take him home to bunk with your blind mule?"

I nodded. "That's exactly what I just said."

"I'll do you one better. I'll come to the vet with you. It'd be good to meet her. We can use my truck to transport the moose to your house. I'll run you back to the shelter later to get your Jeep."

I shrugged. "Fine by me. Kojak can ride in the cab with us. We'll put the moose in the back. I'm sure Kelly has a dog crate large enough to secure him for the short ride."

It made my heart happy to see that Kojak and Houston were getting along so well, and in the short time we'd spent together this afternoon, Houston had relaxed quite a bit. He'd bought two dog beds, one for the living area downstairs and one for his bedroom, but I imagined Kojak might start off on the floor, and I was willing to bet he'd be cuddling with his handsome human in the huge bed that had me enjoying a daydream or two about a cuddle session of my own.

******

"I think the space is organized just fine," I said to Houston later that afternoon, after we'd picked up my still-unnamed moose and were settling him into his new temporary home.

"It makes more sense to have the water trough closer to the back, where it won't make as much of a mess if he spills it," Houston argued.

"Maybe, but it'll be harder to fill. Besides, I'm in here cleaning stalls every day. Even if he spills his water, it won't be a catastrophe. What I'd like to do is figure out how to rig a bottle to a larger canister filled with the milk substitute Kelly gave me. She said the moose needs to eat often. I can't be here to feed him as frequently as he might need, but if I could rig a self-feeder of some sort, I'd just need to fill it two or three times a day."

Houston put his hands on his hips, his right one resting on the butt of his gun, which he seemed to have on his person whether he was on duty or not. "The bottle Kelly gave you is pretty big. It should be easy to secure it so it's accessible on demand. The trick is going to be to keep it filled. Maybe we can use an empty keg from the bar. We can fill it with the milk substitute, hang it high enough so the milk will run down, and then rig a hose from the keg to the bottle that we can secure at a height the moose will find comfortable to feed from."

I smiled. "That's a good idea. I'll call Jake to see if he has an empty one I can have. I have the perfect tubing to use. It should slide right over the bottom of the bottle once I cut a hole in it, forming an airtight seal."

"Taking care of all these animals seems like a huge commitment."

"It is. Not only a time commitment but a financial one as well. Even with a lot of juggling on both accounts, it's been a struggle. That's why I was so grateful to Harley for donating the land and building for the shelter. I really think it's going to make all the difference in terms of the numbers of dogs and cats we can save."

"Are baby moose part of your business plan?" Houston asked as he helped me shovel hay into the stall.

"Not yet. We don't have the staff or infrastructure to take on the rescue and rehabilitation of wild animals, but maybe someday…"

"You're quite a woman, Harmony Carson."

I tried to stifle a smile. "Thanks. You're not too bad yourself." I opened the stall door and left the area now that the moose was settled. "I'm going to take the dogs for a walk. Would you and Kojak like to join us?"

"Do you walk around out in the woods alone every day?"

"Twice a day. But I have seven dogs, so I'm never alone."

"I'm not sure walking around in the forest by yourself is a good idea. At least not until we catch up with Ragland."

"The dogs need exercise and I have seven dogs and a fully loaded rifle. I'll be fine. Having said that, I'd welcome the company. Maybe we can grab a bite on the way back to the shelter to pick up my Jeep."

Houston hesitated, then nodded. "Okay. I'm curious to see how Kojak does with your dogs."

"They'll be fine. Denali is a wolf hybrid who can be cranky at times, but if I tell him to chill, he'll chill. If you want, we can wander over to Ragland's cabin to make sure it's still unoccupied."

"I have my men keeping an eye on the place, but I don't have all that many to go around. As long as I'm here, I wouldn't mind taking a peek. I'll grab my binoculars from the truck."

If Ragland was there, he'd hear eight dogs approaching well before we got close enough to get a peek with binoculars, but I decided not to say as much because checking out the cabin had been my idea in the first place.

"I've been meaning to ask you what you thought about the bomb Ragland tied to Jennifer to create a diversion," I said. "It seems odd to me that he'd have one on hand, ready to go. Our showing up when we did couldn't have been factored into his plan."

"It did seem a bit too convenient. The bomb was a simple device on a timer. Very low tech. If Ragland was Special Forces, I have no doubt he could have known how to build it. I suppose he might have had the bomb on hand in the event he needed it, yet it seems equally likely it was intended to be used as part of some plan that hadn't yet played itself out."

"So he still might be planning to blow something up?"

"It's a possibility."

"Any idea what?" I asked.

"Not a clue."

When we reached the cabin, Houston pulled his gun. The dogs weren't exhibiting any signs of concern, which was enough to convince me the place was empty. The front door was unlocked, and

Houston slowly opened it and went inside. "It's clear," he said after poking his head into every room.

"What about the hidden passage?" I asked.

He led me to a trapdoor in the floor of a closet in one of the bedrooms and pulled it open to expose a dark hole that opened into the passage. "Wait here with the dogs." He pulled a small flashlight out of his pocket, then took a step down. He disappeared for a minute or two, then poked his head back through the opening in the floor. "This is all clear as well. I think the guy is long gone."

I thought about the explosive device he might have had built for some as-yet-unknown reason. "I hope so."

"Let's go back to your place," Houston suggested. "I should check in at the station. It's been fun to play hooky today, but I do have a killer to track down."

I watered the dogs, then had Houston run me back to the shelter to pick up my Jeep. He wanted to check in with his men, so I headed to Neverland to see if Jake had time to help me rig up a feeding system for my newest guest. Jake was an innovator who was good with his hands. The basic concept Houston had come up with was a good one; now I just needed my favorite brother-in-law to turn it into a reality.

******

"So, are you going to continue to call this cute little guy Moose?" Jake asked later that afternoon as he helped me with the feeding system.

"No. He does need a name. He's so little and cute now, but he's going to grow up to be a big bull with a lot of power, so I don't want to stick him with a fluffy name like Honeypot."

Jake laughed. "Honeypot isn't a very manly name. I guess you could just call him Bull."

"I thought of that. And it's still a possibility. I also thought of giving him an Alaskan name, like Kobuk or Valdez." I handed Jake the pair of pliers he'd asked for. "And there are names of towns in Alaska that are common names for males, like Craig or Saint Michael."

"What about Palmer or Anderson?" Jake suggested as he tested the keg we'd rigged to serve as the storage unit for the self-feeder.

"Possibilities as well." I mulled the suggestions over in my mind. Most of the time when it came to naming a new animal in my life, the name came to me fairly easily. "How about Rocky?"

"Rocky was the squirrel," Jake countered.

"So? I like Rocky. It's manly and easy to remember."

Jake shrugged. "Seems like a fine name as long as you aren't going to mind pretty much everyone reminding you that Bullwinkle was the moose and Rocky was the squirrel."

That was true. Still, I liked the name as much as any I'd considered.

"I think this should do it," Jake said, taking a step back.

"We should test it. I'll mix up some of the milk substitute and we'll see if we can get Rocky to drink from it."

"How long until he's on vegetation?" Jake asked.

"Not long. Kelly's going to begin introducing plant-based food next week."

Rocky appeared to be afraid of the strange contraption Jake had spent most of the afternoon building until he realized it produced milk. We'd have to keep an eye on the situation to make sure he didn't overeat, though Kelly didn't think that would be a problem. Besides, Rocky had some catching up to do when it came to overall weight. He was smaller than most newborns, but we'd toughen him up so he could, hopefully, live in the wild one day.

"I need to get back to the bar," Jake said once he was finished. "I asked Wyatt to come in and Sarge is planning to work, so if you need time off to recover from your week, I think we'll be fine without you."

"I'll be in," I said without giving it much thought. "To be perfectly honest, I'm not sure I want to hang out at home alone with nothing to do but stress over whether Ragland has moved on or is still in town, whether he'd done everything he set out to do or there are more victims out there blissfully unaware that he's coming for them."

Chapter 10

It was the dogs barking that woke me from the first deep sleep I'd had in days. I tried to focus on the source of the commotion as I struggled toward wakefulness. "What is it?" I groggily asked as I sat up and tried to get my bearings.

Denali and Yukon were at the back door, barking and growling, and Honey and Lucky were both on the bed with me, both barking as well, and Shia was running around the house barking as if she couldn't quite figure out what it was she was supposed to do.

I grabbed my rifle and stood up. Walking slowly toward the bedroom window, I glanced outside to see something that terrified me more than I could ever imagine. "Oh God," I cried as I ran to the back door. It had only taken a single glance to reveal that the barn was on fire. Without even stopping to put on shoes or a jacket, I ran out into the night. I didn't want the dogs to get hurt in the blaze, so I left them in the house.

As soon as I opened the barn door, Kodi and Juno ran out. They slept in the barn, but they were free to roam the interior and therefore weren't penned. I ran to the pen where Homer was housed and opened the gate to his stall. I clicked a rope to his halter, then picked up the baby moose. Once I had him securely in my arms, I grabbed Homer by the rope and somehow got them both out. I tied Homer to a tree far enough away from the flames so he wouldn't be injured. I wanted to take the moose up to the house, but I needed to go back for the rabbits, so I laid him on the grass and hoped he wouldn't be so terrified he would injure himself even more than he already was by trying to get away.

The smoke was hot and thick by the time I returned for the rabbits. My lungs burned as I opened the door to the cage, then carried them out into the yard one by one. By the time I had them all out, the building was completely enflamed. I let out a sigh of relief and was about to turn to take inventory of the animals I'd just rescued when I felt something stab my back.

"I wondered if you'd be able to save them all before the whole thing went up."

I knew it was Ragland before I turned around. "I should have known it was you. Only a pathetic loser would set fire to a barn full of animals." I tried not to flinch as the barrel of the gun between my shoulder blades was shoved harder into the soft tissue of my back.

"Pretty big speech for a little girl who didn't even take the time to put on shoes."

I clenched my hands when I realized that at some point I'd dropped my rifle. I wondered if it was still in the house or if I'd left it in the barn. I could hear the dogs I'd left in the house barking like crazy, but unfortunately, I wasn't in a position to comfort and reassure them. "The moose. Did you see the moose?"

"Seems to me a baby moose is the least of your problems." The gun was shoved harder into my back. "Now, how about you and I take a little walk?"

Like hell. I was under no illusions that he wouldn't shoot me where I stood if I resisted, but in that moment, I made the decision that if I was going to die, it was going to be in my own yard, protecting the animals I considered family.

"I'm not going anywhere until I make sure the moose is okay. He's just a baby. He'll never survive on his own."

"I can't see that it really matters. There isn't going to be anyone to take care of him if you're dead. Now move."

I could see Kodi and Juno out of the corner of my eye. After they'd run from the fire, they'd headed into the woods. They must have circled back. I wasn't sure what they were going to do, but they were old dogs and I certainly didn't want them getting shot trying to protect me. I was about to call them off when Kodi lunged forward. I didn't have time to think, but my instinct was to whirl around and go for his gun during that split second when Ragland had turned to look at Kodi, taking his attention off me. I threw my weight against the man, who had obviously been caught off guard, sending both of us to the ground. He outweighed me by more than double, so it didn't take him long to pin me beneath himself. I was about to take a bite out of his shoulder when I heard him yell and roll away from me. Somehow, the dogs who had been left indoors had gotten out, and Denali had his neck clenched in his jaws.

I rolled over, grabbed Ragland's gun, and then screamed for Denali to stand down. By this point all seven dogs had encircled the murderer. Teeth bared and growls vibrated on the waves of the silent night, although I noticed the other dogs gave Denali, who was most definitely in charge, plenty of space.

"Detain," I said as loudly and as calmly as I could. I didn't want Denali to back away completely, but I didn't want him to kill Ragland either.

"Get this dog off me," he screamed as Denali loosened his grip on the man's neck but didn't move from his position atop him.

"Shut up or I'll let him finish the job he started."

He visibly surrendered as Denali inched his huge fangs closer to his neck again.

I didn't have my phone with me, but I needed to call Houston. I didn't want to take my attention off Ragland even for a minute, and there was no way Denali was going to let him get to his feet even if I told him to back off completely. I wasn't sure what to do next. I was on the verge of taking a risk and leaving Denali to guard him while I went for the phone when I heard sirens.

Thank God.

The next couple of hours were a blur. One of my neighbors had seen the smoke and called in the fire. Houston appeared to take custody of Ragland, while the volunteer fire department took care of the barn. I closed all the dogs into the bedroom because the back door of the cabin was in shreds; that was how Denali and the others had gotten out. I moved Homer closer to the cabin, then went into the woods to find the baby moose. I just hoped Ragland hadn't cost him his life. I had no idea where the rabbits were, but I'd try to track them down once calm had been restored to my little corner of the world.

"Hey, Rocky, are you out here, little guy?" I was under no illusion that calling the calf would do a bit of good, but it made me feel a bit more in control.

"Harmony?" I heard Jake calling my name.

"Over here," I called back.

Jake came crashing through the brush and wrapped me in a hard hug. "Thank God you're okay. I was terrified when I heard about the fire."

Tears I had been holding at bay began to stream down my cheeks. "The barn is a total loss, the rabbits are gone, and I can't find my moose."

Jake hugged me hard one more time, then took a step back. "I'll help you look for the moose, we'll find the rabbits tomorrow, and I'll make sure the barn is rebuilt just as soon as we can get the materials and the help here to see to it. Where have you already looked for the moose?"

"Just between here and the house."

"Okay." Jake took my hand. "Let's head deeper into the trees. That's where I'd go if I were a baby moose trying to escape a fire."

Chapter 11

Sunday, July 1

It was just over a week since the fire and with a grateful heart I hosted a party to thank the dozens of volunteers who'd helped to rebuild my barn. Not only was the new barn bigger and better than the old one, but Jake had ordered a special feeding system from a large dairy that regularly bottle-fed their calves. Rocky was doing well on a diet of local vegetation Kelly had weaned him on to, but Jake figured as long as we were rebuilding the barn, we may as well build in the feeding system, which could be used to nurse any new roommates Homer and Rocky might have in the future.

It had been a difficult week for sure, but as promised on the night of the fire, Jake had helped me find Rocky, who was terrified but otherwise unharmed. And the following day, after things had calmed down a bit, he'd helped me track down the rabbits too. When I'd first adopted them, they'd been hurt and in need of medical care. Although they were perfectly healthy now and might very well be fine in the wild, they'd been in captivity for so long, I wasn't certain they'd have the instincts necessary to protect themselves.

Denali had been on edge since the night he'd taken down Ragland, but the other dogs were acting as if nothing intense had ever happened. Kodi and Juno had been forced to sleep in the house while the barn was being rebuilt, but I had a feeling that once it was ready to move in to, they'd be just as happy to bunk with Homer again.

Ragland had been arrested and transferred to Anchorage. I knew a trial was quite a ways off, given the complexities of the situation, but in the meantime he was in jail and unlikely to see freedom in his lifetime. I was sorry someone hadn't been on to him sooner, before he killed Pastor Brown and Diane and left Silvia injured. But part of doing what the team and I do means having to live with the fact that, as much as we wish it were otherwise, we can't save everyone.

"I have to hand it to you: The residents of Rescue really know how to get something done," Houston said when he came into the kitchen, where I was putting the finishing touches on the potato salad I was serving with the chicken and ribs the guys were grilling.

"Rescue might be a small town, but it's a small town with heart. We're like a big family. If one member has a need, everyone pitches in to make sure it's met. Can you grab that pan of baked beans, please?"

Houston picked up the beans and followed me to the table where I'd been setting out food for the past half hour. "You make a good point about the willingness of a lot of folks who live in small towns to pitch in and help their neighbors, but if you'd told me a few days ago that you'd have a functioning barn by the end of the week, I would have thought you were crazy."

"Building a barn may be a big job for one or two people, but when fifty friends and neighbors show up to help, the job becomes a whole lot smaller. If you don't mind following me back to the kitchen to get the slaw, I'll grab the bread, and I think we'll be ready for the meat. By the way, how are things working out with Kojak?"

"Better than I could ever have hoped. Sure, he's pretty much convinced he's the king of my house and I'm his loyal servant, but he's a well-behaved dog with a gentle disposition and I'm thoroughly enjoying his company. I'm not sure he'll ever be a real police dog—he doesn't seem to have that killer instinct—but I've been taking him to work with me, and he's very willing to do what I say and stay out of the way. Everyone loves him. In fact, we have folks stopping by the station every day to bring him a toy or a treat. I think having him ride along with me is good for morale."

I smiled as I opened the oven and slid out the bread. "I'm really glad things worked out. Having a dog really is the answer to a lot of life's little problems."

"I suppose when you have a wolf hybrid who doesn't hesitate to take down a man with a gun to save your life, that's really true. If there was ever a dog perfect for police work, it would be Denali."

"Not necessarily," I said as I began to slice the bread. "Denali is very brave and strong and protective, but he's also very alpha. You need a dog who'll listen to you and do as you say, no matter what. Your life as well as his could depend on it."

"Yeah. I guess I can see that. I'm going to take this slaw out and check on the dogs. The last time I saw Kojak, he was playing with your dogs, but I want to be sure he hasn't wandered off."

After Houston left to check on the dogs, I placed the bread in a basket, then opened the refrigerator to look for the fruit salad I'd forgotten to set out. I grabbed the bowl and was turning around when someone walked up behind me. I guess I must still have been skittish from my encounter with Ragland because I let out a little scream and dropped the bowl.

"Are you okay?"

"Harley?" I put a hand over my pounding heart.

"I didn't mean to scare you. Here, let me help you with that." Harley grabbed some paper towels and began cleaning up the fruit that had landed on the floor.

"It's okay." I bent down next to him, our hands brushing as we both scooped up fruit. "I'm really glad to see you. I guess I'm just a bit skittish after everything that has happened the past couple of weeks."

"That's totally understandable. I should have realized and made a point to make more noise when I came in."

I dumped the fruit we'd scooped up into the sink and went for the mop. "It wasn't you. Really. It's me. I thought you couldn't come for at least another week."

"I thought so too," he said as he took the mop from my hands and took over cleaning the floor. "I just woke up yesterday morning and realized I couldn't deal with LA one more day. I booked an overnight flight and here I am."

"To stay?" I asked as I washed my hands, then wiped down the counter.

"For a while. I'm anxious to see how things are going at the shelter, but I'm even more anxious to hear what's been going on here. I've picked up little snippets here and there, but I'd love to get the whole story from you."

"And I'd like to tell you. After I feed the fifty or so people who have given up their weekend to build me a barn. If you want to grab a bite with us, I can fill you in while we do the dishes."

A thoughtful expression crossed Harley's face. "Do you have any idea how long it's been since I've washed a sinkful of dishes?"

"Was it presumptuous of me to suggest you might want to?"

Harley smiled. He set the mop aside and took my hand in his. Then he paused and looked me directly in the eye. "There's nothing in the world I'd enjoy more than washing dishes with the stunningly beautiful woman I can't stop thinking about and I find to be more and more amazing every time I speak to her."

Now that, I decided, was how you deliver a closing line.

USA Today best-selling author Kathi Daley lives in beautiful Lake Tahoe with her husband Ken. When she isn't writing, she likes spending time hiking the miles of desolate trails surrounding her home. She has authored more than a hundred and fifty books in thirteen series. Find out more about her books at **www.kathidaley.com**

Printed in Great Britain
by Amazon